THE SECRET PASSAGE

by Kathleen Pennell

illustrated by
Lauren Pennell

THE SECRET PASSAGE
PONY INVESTIGATORS #5

Copyright © 2005
by
Paddock Publishing
26 Cedar Lane
Lancaster, PA 17601

Library of Congress Number: 2005908623
International Standard Book Number: 1-932864-42-3

Printed 2005 by
Masthof Press
219 Mill Road
Morgantown, PA 19543-9516

Dedicated

to

my sister, traveling companion, and friend,

Karen McGillivray

Special thanks to:

Mrs. Joyce Anderson, Millersville University

for her invaluable help in editing this book

Devon Capizi

of Lancaster Country Day School

Tyler Chadwick

suggestion for title of book

Dr. Todd Trout

technical advice

Dr. Carrie Ullmer

technical advice

Contents

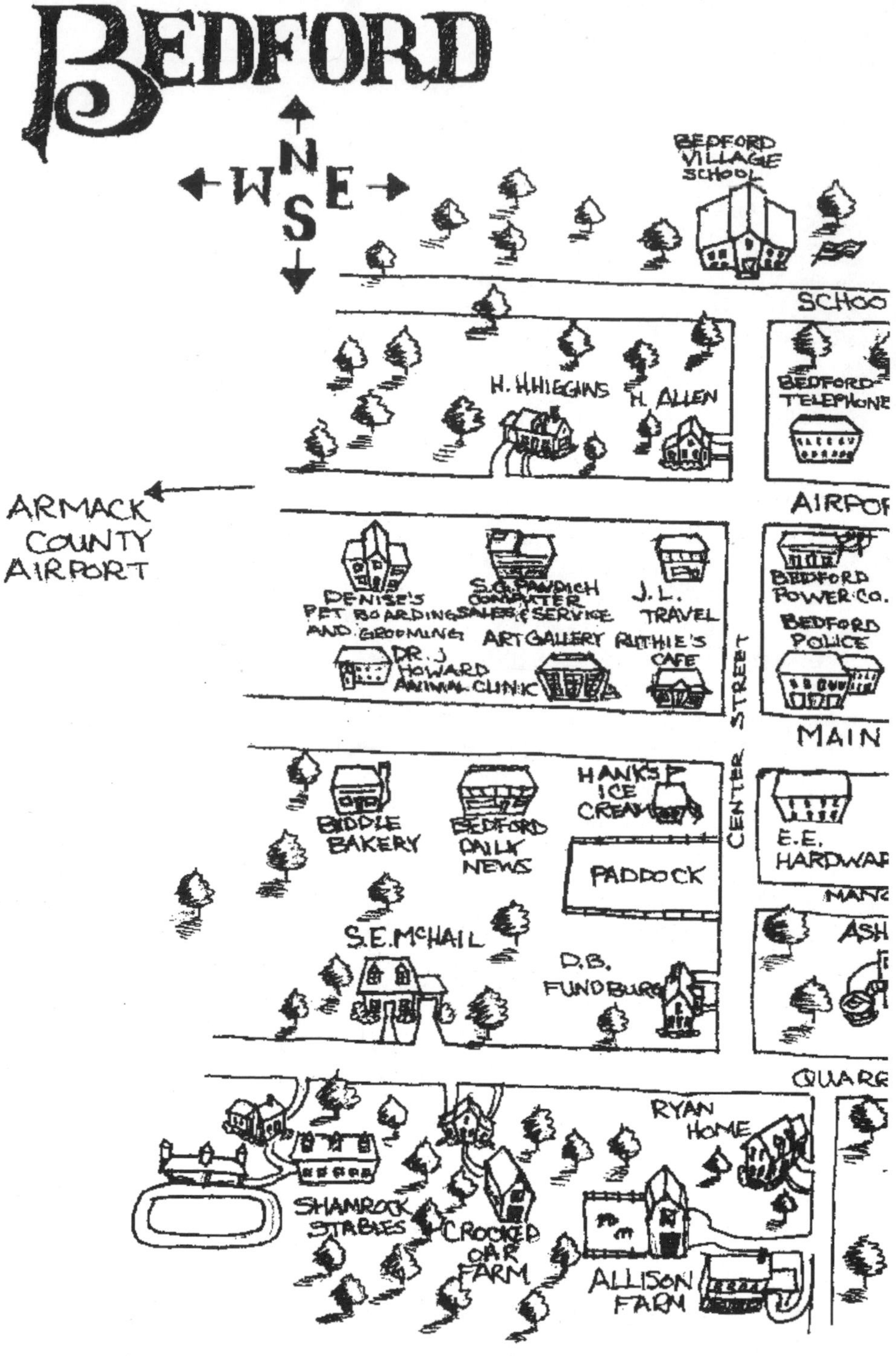
BEDFORD
N
W
E
S
BEDFORD VILLAGE SCHOOL
SCHOO
H. H HIGGINS
H. ALLEN
BEDFORD TELEPHONE
ARMACK COUNTY AIRPORT
AIRPOR
DENISE'S PET BOARDING AND GROOMING
S.G. SANDICH COMPUTER SALES & SERVICE
J.L. TRAVEL
BEDFORD POWER CO.
BEDFORD POLICE
DR. J HOWARD ANIMAL CLINIC
ART GALLERY
RUTHIE'S CAFE
CENTER STREET
MAIN
HANK'S ICE CREAM
BIDDLE BAKERY
BEDFORD DAILY NEWS
PADDOCK
E.E. HARDWAR
S.E. McHAIL
D.B. FUNDBURG
ASH
QUARR
RYAN HOME
SHAMROCK STABLES
CROOKED OAR FARM
ALLISON FARM

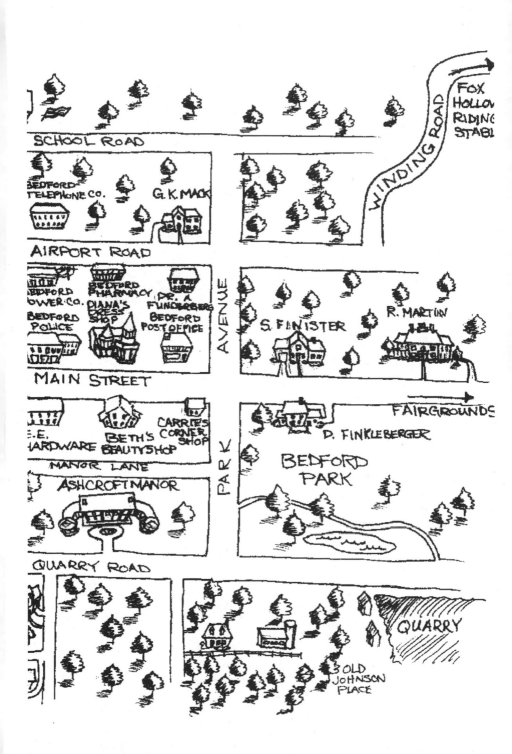

Chapter 1

The Plane

The plane dropped one thousand feet. Downdrafts were hard on the nerves not to mention the stomach. A fickle westerly wind kept Hunter's foot constantly on the foot pedals, easing the plane back on its course. It was a bad night to be flying. In five minutes he would be there. The engine lost a little power as he pulled back on the throttle. At one thousand feet above ground level, the aircraft broke through the dark, billowing clouds. Leaning forward he peered out of the front window. Just ahead were the silos. The airstrip was supposed to be right next to it, but the strip of lights wasn't on yet so he couldn't land. He drummed his fingertips on the top of the throttle knob. It wasn't easy to look over the nose of the plane.

The expression on Hunter's face darkened. What a night to be out flying, he muttered for the tenth time. They called him away from his dinner table at the last minute. His wife and son were used to it. An hour later he was in the air. If the airline hadn't axed his job, he wouldn't need to do this. With the boy sick and his wife staying home with him, money was tight. Tonight's job was easy money, and he couldn't pass it up. But, there was something not quite right about this whole thing. That's how his life had been lately, not quite right.

Hunter turned the wheel slightly to the left pressing his broad shoulder to the metal frame. The plane tipped over just enough to allow him to see more ground below. He arched his neck closer to the window. "Where are the lights?" He growled angrily under his breath. "I can't land without the lights." The palms of his hands were sweaty as he gripped the wheel. If the lights didn't appear soon, he'd have to swing around for another pass. Suddenly, a parallel string of lights popped through the darkness. "About time," he said, wiping his brow with the sleeve of his shirt. Hunter wanted to be home by 11:00. That gave him two hours.

The string of lights ran directly in front of him. Hunter continued to pull back on the throttle with his right hand while he kept his left hand on the wheel. The plane dropped to three hundred feet above ground level. The wind gusted slightly. He corrected with the foot pedals. Two hundred feet, one hundred feet . . . he flared the plane by gently pulling back on the wheel at the last second, then the wheels touched the ground. Hunter stepped on the brake and brought the plane to a standstill. The double row of lights went out. The pilot flipped off the lights in the cockpit. He sat in complete darkness.

The mounting tension of the last fifteen minutes melted away in layers. The last layer was reserved for when he was airborne again. Slowly, Hunter let out his breath and sank back in his seat. If the money weren't great, he'd never do this again. He shouldn't do it again anyway. It just didn't feel right. Why did it always come down to money? He shook the nerves out of his lean body. Sliding over to the passenger side, Hunter got out, climbed over the wing, then opened up the cargo area. He lifted two thin, rectangular packages out of safekeeping and secured the cargo door.

From out of the dark, a man approached. Fifty feet away, Hunter heard the deep cough and the rasp in his breathing. Two hands reached out to take the packages Hunter held. The man stood still until Hunter turned away from him. After the man checked the seal to make sure no tampering had taken place, he slit along the edges of the packages. His breathing quickened and the rasp became even more apparent. The man turned on a flashlight long enough to make sure of the packages' contents, then took them some distance away behind a small bush. He picked up an envelope stuffed with hundred dollar bills.

Hunter grimaced in disgust as he heard the man stumbling back to the plane. It was always the same. Everything had to be counted and verified . . . always making sure everything was just right. No one knew anyone else in the network. Nobody trusted anybody. Each person had only his part to play; otherwise the entire operation could fall like a row of dominoes.

Hunter leaned against the plane, but straightened up when he heard nearing footsteps. The envelope was deposited into Hunter's hands, then it was his turn to tear something open and check its contents. He slowly counted the bills, nodded his head, and stuffed the envelope inside his jacket. There was never a handshake or conversation. It would be impossible to identify each other if it ever came to that. It was just a business exchange, then life returned to normal until the next time.

Hunter slipped behind the controls of the plane. He flipped on the lights again and started the engine. After Hunter taxied to the end of the grass strip, he turned into the wind for takeoff. Hunter sat impatiently for a moment until the double row of lights was turned on. Then, with his right hand, Hunter shoved the throttle in. The engine roared as the plane raced bumpily down the makeshift runway. The pilot pulled back slightly on the wheel, and the plane lifted off the ground. Within one minute, Hunter and the plane had disappeared into the clouds again. He'd be home by 11:00 p.m.

The man coughed into his arm as he deposited the double strip of lights into a large bag. The rectangular packages he secured under his arm. Picking up both items he began to walk. Then, suddenly, he just disappeared.

A hundred feet from where the plane had landed and taken off a young girl sat on her bicycle in a state of shock. Maybe it was an alien from outer space. She'd seen movies like this. Except this was a normal plane. And even though it was dark and she couldn't see who it was, she did see the outlines of two real people, at least they looked real. Except, one of them had just vanished. A ghost?! Ghosts only happened in movies, didn't they? What happened before her eyes completely baffled and frightened her more than a little. Nobody would believe her. She tended to stretch the truth a bit . . . just occasionally. She better not say anything. She might get into trouble, but on the way home she continued to wonder. . . .

*   *   *   *

Amy Jo and Becky ambled down Center Street on their ponies, Ginger Snap and Oreo Cookie. No rush to be at work any special time, so they were headed for Hank's Ice Cream Shop. This was the first job they'd had all summer where it

4

didn't matter what time they got there. Nobody was going to check up on them. Might as well enjoy some ice cream and then go to work.

"Hank better not be out of chocolate chip cookie dough again," Amy Jo announced. "If he is, it will make three times this month that he's been out of my favorite flavor."

Becky shook her head. "Yesterday was the first time all summer Hank was out of your flavor," she informed her friend.

"Oh, no it wasn't," Amy Jo quickly reminded her. "When we were at the circus, he ran out."

"Yeah, but Hank had just left to pick up more at the store. He was back in half an hour."

"Well . . ." Amy Jo struggled to counter Becky's defense. "So, okay, yesterday was the first time, but he'd better have it today."

The girls rode their ponies with loose reins. Ginger and Oreo knew where they were headed. This was the ice cream hour and both mares had their own favorite flavors. The ponies stopped in front of Hank's paddock before the girls had a chance to rein them in.

Becky leaned over and unlatched the catch on the gate. The gate swung open and the ponies stepped inside. Ginger and Oreo danced a bit as their tack was taken off. Their eyes were focused a hundred feet away on the lush grass. The minute the saddles and bridles were removed, the mares trotted away to their favorite spot under a nearby tree, then switched their tails as they lowered their heads. An overhead bell jingled as the girls walked through the door.

"Hey, girls," Hank smiled as Amy Jo and Becky walked up to the stools in front of the counter. Hank was above medium height, slender, yet well-muscled and athletic looking. "Before you start in on me, Amy Jo, I've got chocolate chip cookie dough, okay."

Amy Jo's eyes lit up. "In that case, I'll have double what I usually get to make up for yesterday."

"Double it is," Hank said, his chocolatey skin crinkling around his dark eyes. "How about you, Becky? Same as usual?"

"Yes, please," replied Becky politely.

"Gottcha," Hank picked up the ice cream scooper flipped it into the air and caught it deftly on its way down. "One double chocolate chip cookie dough and one regular fudge ripple coming up." He glanced over his shoulder while he got Amy Jo's double order. "I suppose you'll be wanting ice cream for your ponies when you leave, right?"

"Right," said Becky.

"They'd stage a revolt if we forgot," Amy Jo added.

Hank placed their ice cream in front of them. "You know Devon Capizi from school?" he asked, setting spoons and napkins down before them. "Couple years older than you, I think."

"Yeah, she's going into eighth grade. I know her. She's the pitcher on the softball team. They always say, 'Devon Capizi, toss it nice and easy.'" Amy Jo explained the little rhyme. "What about her?" her detective instinct asked.

Hank grinned. This was one girl who got to the bottom of every situation. "She's going to be working for me for a few weeks. Been in here every morning since last week for training," he explained. "I need to help my dad for a while in the afternoons. He broke his leg," he added before Amy Jo had a chance to ask what was wrong with him.

Becky looked up sympathetically. "I hope it wasn't a bad break."

"No," Hank shook his head. "Doc says it'll heal pretty quick, but he's gotta stay off of it. And my Mom's sure got her hands full when Dad wants to be out in the shop doing stuff."

Behind them the bell over the door jingled as Devon walked through. "Hi, Hank," she said as she walked behind the counter.

"Hi, yourself," he answered as he took his apron off. "Thanks for coming in early. I want to run across the street to the art gallery for a few minutes before I leave town."

"Art gallery?" Amy Jo asked. "Anything new there?"

"Oh, yeah!" Hank exclaimed. "Virginia's got a ton of stuff in on loan from some big galleries in New York."

"Wow," Becky breathed softly. "I didn't know that a little place like Bedford would have important art work."

"It's Virginia's doing," Hank explained. "She went to art school in New York and knows a bunch of important people. Paintings just started coming in this week. She expects to draw people from all over to look at it. Anyway, I thought I'd drop over there before I run out to see my folks."

"How did you know about it?" demanded Amy Jo. "It wasn't in the paper."

"Virginia told me last week when she was in here. She likes ice cream, too." Hank picked up his keys and slid from behind the counter. "Anyway," he added, tossing his keys in the air then catching them behind his back. "It'll be in tomorrow's paper."

"Looks like I missed out on that one," Amy Jo grumbled to herself.

Hank smiled widely and winked at Becky. It was rare that he was privy to information ahead of Amy Jo. "See ya, girls," he called over his shoulder as he walked through the door.

"Bye, Hank," said Becky.

"Bye, Hank," called Amy Jo. "Thanks for not being out of chocolate chip cookie dough."

"Right," he laughed as he shut the door.

"So, what's new," Devon asked, drawing a clean apron over her head. "Caught any dangerous criminals lately?" Her dark blue eyes sparkled mischievously.

"Got an easy job this time," answered Amy Jo, ignoring the little dig.

"Finally!" said Becky with a shudder.

"So, what are you doing?" Devon pressed.

"We're housesitting," Becky announced between bites. "We have to take in the newspaper and the mail, water the plants, feed the cat, and check the freezer to make sure it still works."

Devon looked puzzled. "Why do you have to check the freezer?"

Amy Jo swallowed her ice cream before she answered. "They've got lots of food in there. It would spoil if the freezer stopped working."

Devon nodded her head. "Okay. So, where will you be housesitting?"

"It's the Funderburg place," said Amy Jo as she wiped her mouth with a napkin.

"Just in back of Hank's shop on Center Street," Becky added.

Devon nodded her head at Amy Jo, then at Becky. "I should have guessed."

Becky's spoon stopped midway to her  mouth. "Why is that?" she asked, spilling drops of fudge ripple on the counter.

"Mrs. Funderburg was in here earlier in the week with her three little girls. She had matching yellow sundresses on them and they all wanted chocolate ice cream. She mentioned something about taking a vacation," said Devon as she mopped up the spilled ice cream.

Amy Jo put down her spoon. "Chocolate ice cream and sundresses can be a dangerous combination."

Devon rinsed out her cloth in the sink. "Oh, Mrs. Funderburg came prepared," she began. "She had bibs for all of them."

Devon frowned to herself as she absently wiped the same spot on the counter.

Amy Jo studied her and finally said, "Everything okay?"

Devon stopped mopping away and looked up. "Sure . . . sure."

Amy Jo studied her for a moment, then asked again. "So everything's okay?"

Devon looked out the window at the sidewalk. "Sure," she said again.

Amy Jo and Becky exchanged glances.

"So, why don't you tell us about all this okay stuff," said Amy Jo casually.

"Well," Devon absently rinsed the cloth again in a nearby sink. "My Dad works night shift at the power plant. Since we live out in the country near Armack Airport, he goes to work in Bedford by taking Quarry Road to Center Street."

When she stopped talking, Amy Jo leaned forward. "Okay, I know where you live and that your Dad works second shift at the power plant."

"Well," Devon began. "Second shift means he works 3:00 in the afternoon until 11:00 at night. So, a couple of nights ago, I had to take Dad's lunch box to him on my bike and was heading back home." She looked at the girls to see if they were following her train of thought.

Amy Jo and Becky stopped eating their ice cream and leaned forward at attention. They both raised their eyebrows encouragingly.

Devon started mopping the same clean spot again. "Well, you know we live close to the airport, and I watch airplanes come and go all the time."

"I like to watch airplanes, too," Becky agreed.

Devon decided that she may as well lay the whole thing out and get it over with. "Okay, the other night I was heading back on my bike, and I wasn't even near the airport. But, I heard this airplane flying in real low. So, I pulled my bike off the road and pedaled onto a grassy field. And you'll never believe what happened," she said, her courage suddenly failing.

"What?" both girls said at once.

Devon leaned forward. The three noses were only inches apart. "I saw a plane land in a field.

CHAPTER 2

The Fourth Room

The girls all sat back. No one spoke for over a moment. Devon continued. "There was a double row of lights to show the pilot where to land. Then, when the plane was on the ground, the lights went off. The pilot got out and handed a package to somebody, then took off again." She looked down at the counter, held her breath, and waited.

"Where did it happen?" asked Amy Jo.

Devon's shoulders relaxed. They believed her so far, but she hadn't told them the strangest part of it yet. "Just a little ways out of town off Quarry Road. You know where those three big silos are?"

The girls nodded their heads.

"Well, it was just past that. It was in a field back off the road. Far enough that you wouldn't notice it from Quarry Road if you were in a car with the engine running and the windows up, but I was on my bike, so I heard it."

Amy Jo thought for a moment. "The pilot gave somebody a package and then took off again?"

Devon nodded her head. "That's all he did. The plane was only on the ground for a couple of minutes. But," she continued hesitantly, "something else happened."

Amy Jo eyed Devon closely. "Like what?"

Devon cleared her throat. "Well, after the plane took off, this guy was standing there stuffing the lights into some kind of bag or something. And, all of a sudden, he just disappeared." She waited for a moment looking from one girl to the other. Neither girl said anything.

Becky took another bite of ice cream. "That *is* really strange. No wonder you're upset."

Devon sighed with relief. Somebody understood how she felt. "Yeah, it was definitely weird all right."

The remainder of Amy Jo's ice cream had turned to soup. "Have you told anybody else about this?" she asked.

"No, it's too weird. I wasn't sure anyone would believe me," remarked Devon. "Especially the part about the man disappearing. I mean there are bushes and trees and everything, but one minute he was there and the next he was gone."

Amy Jo frowned slightly as she slid off her stool. "Maybe we'll ride out there later today or tomorrow and take a look around," she said. "We'll let you know if we find anything."

"Thanks," said Devon as she removed the girls' empty bowls and wiped the counter with her cloth.

Becky suddenly remembered the ponies. "We need some ice cream for Ginger and Oreo."

With the relief of having unburdened this strange event, Devon looked at the girls with amusement. "You buy ice cream for your horses?"

"They're ponies," Becky corrected, "and they love ice cream."

Devon giggled. "Did your horses put in a request for their favorite flavor?" she asked, her natural exuberance taking over. "One hoof tap for vanilla or two hoof taps for chocolate."

14

Amy Jo rolled her eyes. "Ginger likes vanilla and Oreo likes strawberry."

Devon continued to giggle as she dipped up the cones. "Sorry, I laughed," she said as she brought them to the counter. "I've been in a goofy mood ever since I saw that airplane." She was feeling a little ashamed that she'd teased them about their ponies after the girls had agreed to help.

"No, sweat," said Amy Jo, taking a cone. "We understand."

Becky reached for the strawberry cone. "We'll see you tomorrow," she said, her eyes smiling with understanding. "Maybe we'll know something about the plane then."

The girls paid for the ice cream, said their goodbyes, and headed back to the paddock with the ponies' cones.

As soon as the two friends rounded the corner, Oreo and Ginger shot over to the fence. The mares whinnied softly. They stood nodding their heads, nudging each other for first place. Amy Jo and Becky opened the gate and stepped through. Ginger and Oreo ate the ice cream, cones and all. They licked around their muzzles, then started in on any residue of ice cream left on the girls' hands even in between their fingers.

Usually, there was laughter between the girls as they watched their ponies devour their ice cream. Today, they were silent.

"Why would somebody choose a field to land a plane when the airport is only a couple miles away?" asked Amy Jo.

Oreo had finished her cone and was sniffing around Becky for candy. "The guy vanishing into thin air is what makes me nervous."

"There's got to be a simple answer for that. We just don't know what it is yet," said Amy Jo as her chestnut pony nosed the other hand looking for more ice cream. Amy Jo smiled slightly as she watched the mare's head drop in disappointment.

"This started out to be a nice day, too," Becky began. "And now look what's happening."

"You ought to look on the bright side of things for once, Beck."

"Like what?" answered Becky while her pony sniffed away at her pocket.

"Well . . ." Amy Jo struggled. "We've got an easy job at the Funderburgs'. We don't have to get up early. And when we go out to investigate about this plane business, nobody will be there."

The look on Becky's face didn't look too hopeful. "Yeah, I guess you're right," she finally said.

Ginger and Oreo had licked off everything that smelled of ice cream, poked around the girls' pockets sniffing for treats, and now shook their heads in disappointment. Ginger rested her head on Amy Jo's shoulder. Oreo gave Becky a little shove in the direction of the gate. Becky tapped her pony's nose to remind the mare that shoving was not allowed. Oreo stood still, then leaned toward Becky asking for her favorite spot to be scratched.

Becky's eyes lit up as she turned to her friend. "Why don't we go to the art gallery for a few minutes and see what's there? We can stop at the Funderburg house on our way back."

Amy Jo thought for a moment. Art wasn't her thing, but maybe knowing something about art might come in handy someday. "Okay," she said with a shrug. "We can't take the ponies."

"They'll have more fun here anyway,"
Becky agreed.

The ponies stood at the gate until the girls walked away. They neighed, and their eyes followed Amy Jo and Becky for the first minute. When it became obvious to Ginger and Oreo that they were not going with the girls, the mares turned around and walked back to their grazing spot under the tree.

Amy Jo and Becky strolled up Center Street, turned left onto Main Street, and walked into the art gallery.

Virginia Delmay was in the front room organizing a display for several pieces of artwork that had arrived that morning. There were code numbers on each identification tag which matched the painting to the place from which it was borrowed.

Miss Delmay's long, dark hair covered her pale skin as she leaned over to study the cards describing the paintings. At the sound of the door closing, she looked up and smiled. "Hello, girls," she said, straightening up. Her large blue-gray eyes looked curiously at Amy Jo. "Why, Amy Jo, I had no idea that you were interested in art."

"Well," Amy Jo struggled with the truth. "I thought I might learn something."

Virginia nodded her head at Amy Jo's honesty. "Admirable idea," she said, then turned to Becky "Your family just moved here not long ago, didn't they?" she asked.

"Yes, earlier in the summer," Becky answered.

Virginia's mouth turned up and her eyes sparkled. "And did you come in here to learn something as well?" Virginia asked teasingly.

"Oh, no ma'am," said Becky. "What I mean is, I came because I like art."

Virginia laughed easily. "That's wonderful. I am delighted that both of you came by." She raised both hands up in the air. "Some of the paintings are still in boxes, but if you don't mind the mess, you are welcome to stroll through the rooms and see what is hanging. You'll have the place to yourself. Hank was here a short time ago, but he only had a few minutes."

They passed through into the second room stopping to look at each piece. The modern, abstract paintings hung in the third room. These paintings were mostly splashes of colors. The artists' intent was lost on the girls. They walked slowly from painting to painting trying to guess what the artist had in mind until they came to the last one which was beside the doorway leading to the fourth room.

Amy Jo twisted her head from side to side. "Hm," she said.

"This one came from somewhere in New York City," said Becky reading the identification card beside the painting. "I was there one time."

Amy Jo scratched the back of her head. "Been to the art gallery in New York City, have you?" she inquired, checking out the series of letters and numbers written on the identification card. "So, I suppose you've met some of these weirdo painters, right?"

Becky stretched her arms in front of herself and created a rectangular frame with her hands as she studied the painting. "I've met one or two of them. They're not weird, just interesting and unique," she answered as she continued to tilt her head. "The painting looks a little . . . ," she was at a loss for words.

Amy Jo watched her friend for a moment, then copied the rectangular shape with her own hands as she studied

18

the painting. "Yeah, it's definitely that all right," she finally commented.

As they stood there, the sound of heavy, raspy breathing followed by a deep series of coughs came from the fourth room. The girls looked at each other. They hadn't heard a sound coming from that room until now. In fact, they hadn't heard anybody in the entire gallery until now. Where did this person come from?

Amy Jo looked at Becky, then whispered. "I thought Miss Delmay said nobody was here, but us."

Becky suddenly lost all interest in the painting in front of her. "That's what she told us all right," she whispered back, looking over her shoulder at the exit sign.

Amy Jo grabbed hold of the corner of the doorway and edged nearer until her eyes were level with the opening. She peeked around the corner. The raspy breathing continued, but nobody was in sight.

CHAPTER 3

Charlotte

Amy Jo eased away from the door, then turned to Becky. She jerked her head towards the next room. "Let's see what's in here," she mouthed the words.

Becky swallowed and eyed the exit sign again. "It's the last room, right?" she asked.

"Right, last room."

They stood in the archway of the door. The room was the largest of the four, and there were a number of standing displays throughout the room from which paintings were hung. The raspy breathing and coughing continued from the right at the far end of the room, but several standing displays blocked the view of whomever it was.

The girls turned to the left and began viewing the paintings on the walls and the standing displays. They worked their way towards the far end of the room closer to the person who appeared unable to take a breath without racking coughs.

The girls looked at each other. Nobody in Bedford had that kind of rasp or cough. It was definitely an outsider. They moved on to the next two paintings.

Amy Jo leaned in closer for a better look. "You know I like this room better than the other one," she began. "At least the paintings look like something I know."

"Well, everyone likes different things," Becky countered.

Amy Jo stood with one hand on her hip and the other one pointing to different parts of the painting. "You take this one right here," she said, indicating the painting in front of them. "Now, I can tell that this is a painting of two girls. The blond one is playing the piano and the dark haired one is leaning over her watching her play. You don't have to sit around and guess what it's all about. I always say it doesn't seem too hard to just slap some paint onto a canvas and everybody thinks it's great, but nobody knows what it is. I mean I could do that."

"There's a lot more to it than that," Becky began. "I mean there's the development of space and use of color, and well, I don't know. Everybody likes different things."

"I'll say they do," Amy Jo responded. "I like rooms two and four, but I can't even tell you what room three is."

As they neared the last standing display, they realized that they hadn't heard any raspy breathing or hacking cough for at least a minute. They rounded the last standing display. The room was empty.

The girls listened, then retraced their steps throughout the room. There was no chance that the person had escaped. There was only one door in and out of the room and that door lead to the rest of the gallery.

Becky looked at Amy Jo. "I don't get it," she said. "Where did he go?"

Amy Jo studied the wall behind the last display. There was paneling running about four feet up the wall, but the space above the paneling was smooth with no possible in-dication of a doorway.

"I'm going to start on this side," began Amy
Jo heading to the right. "You look over there," she
continued, nodding her head toward the left.

"What are we looking for?" asked Becky
quizzically.

Amy Jo looked up in surprise. "For a sliver of an outline
which indicates the presence of a door."

"Okay," said Becky as she squatted down to run her
hand over the paneling. Several minutes later she frowned
as she heard Amy Jo pounding away on the wood. "What
are you doing now?" she hissed, then peeked around the
corner of the displays to make sure no one was coming to
warn them off.

"Hollow," muttered Amy Jo as she shifted her
position.

"Hollow?" answered Becky. "Is that all you can say
. . . hollow?"

Amy Jo began to pound in the new spot. "Yeah, I'm
checking to see if there's a hollow-sounding place on the
paneling. Might mean a door."

"Well, do you think you could check a little more quietly?" Becky began to edge toward the exit. "Anyway, I
think it's time to go to the Funderburg's house."

"Oh, well, can't find anything," said Amy Jo as she
turned on her heel and followed Becky to the front of the
gallery. "May as well go."

As they neared the front room, Amy Jo whispered to
her friend. "Let's ask Miss Delmay if she's sure no one
else was here."

"Why should we ask her?" Becky countered. "She already said we were the only ones here besides Hank."

"Well, maybe she'll remember someone if we press her."

Becky looked at her pal in dismay. "This is not a case, and we are not going to interrogate Miss Delmay."

Amy Jo dropped her shoulders. "We're not going to tie her to a chair and shine a bright light in her eyes. We're just going to sort of . . . ask her in a passing way."

"Whatever."

"Whatever?!" asked Amy Jo. "When did you pick up that word? You're watching too many of those snotty shows on TV."

Miss Delmay was setting the last painting in place as the girls came into the first room.

Amy Jo walked up to Miss Delmay, but waited until the lady turned to them. "I was just wondering if somebody came in just before we did?" she asked.

Miss Delmay widened her eyes in curiosity. "Why, no, only Hank, but then he left before you got here. He didn't have much time," she explained again. "Why do you ask?"

Becky stepped forward. "We thought we heard someone in the back room," she explained.

Miss Delmay looked puzzled. "There's only one way in and out of here and that is through the front door," she said, pointing to the door behind where the girls stood. "I really am not officially open," she continued. "Hank and you two girls are the only ones who have been here all day." Then, shifting gears, Miss Delmay asked, "Did you girls enjoy yourselves?"

"Oh, yes, ma'am," said Becky quickly.

"Yes, ma'am," echoed Amy Jo.

The girls stood still for a moment not knowing quite what else to say. Mumbling their thanks they left. They were silent as they crossed Main Street.

24

"Who could it possibly have been?" Amy Jo muttered out loud.

Becky shook her head. "No idea," she answered.

Amy Jo pressed on. "I mean Miss Delmay said nobody was there, so who was it?"

"Well, somebody was definitely there," stated Becky. "The question is, how did he get in that room without first coming through the front door?"

"And how could he leave so quietly that neither of us could hear a door open or close?" Amy Jo replied pointedly.

The girls continued down Center Street until they came to the front yard of the Funderburg house.

"Have you got the key?" asked Becky as they strolled up the front walk.

Amy Jo shook herself awake. She was still puzzled by the man in the gallery. "Uh, Mr. Funderburg said that the key would be on a hook in the backyard. It's on one of those bug zapper poles," she answered as she skirted the porch and headed for the backyard.

The yard was a large one with trees, shrubs, and flowers planted in groups. The bug zapper was off to the side somewhat hidden by shrubs.

Amy Jo squatted down in back of the pole. "Ah, here's the key," she said as she grabbed it off the hook.

The girls retraced their steps to the front. They hopped up to the front porch and inserted the key into the door.

The girls stepped into the hallway and looked around. It was a spacious older house with a long central hallway running from front to back. If they walked straight ahead past the stairway, they would reach a door which led to the backyard. From the hallway, the girls saw two rooms on the left. On the right

25

side, there was a door in front of the stairway and one on the far side of the stairway.

The kitchen was the second door on the right located behind the stairway. Its door swung on hinges so that if you weren't careful, it could hit you in the face after the person in front of you had already walked through. The cat was under the table. Her name was Charlotte.

"Completely black," said Amy Jo as she stared at her from a distance.

"She must be named after the black spider in *Charlotte's Web*," Becky commented.

Amy Jo looked at Becky curiously. "Why would they name a cat after a crumby old spider?" she asked.

"Well," said Becky turning around. "They make a point of saying that the spider in *Charlotte's Web* is black. And this cat is completely black."

"She's black all right," agreed Amy Jo heading for the cupboard where the cat food was supposed to be held.

"I wonder if she's friendly?" Becky murmured to herself.

"I wouldn't count on it," said Amy Jo. "When I talked with Mr. Funderburg on the phone, he made a point of saying that we should feed her and then stand back."

"Oh," Becky sounded disappointed. "That's too bad. Maybe we can make friends with her." She squatted down and peered through the table legs at the cat.

"This is one time I intend to follow orders." It was her way of warning her partner.

Becky leaned forward and made little cooing sounds.

Charlotte stared unblinkingly at her with green eyes, the color of pears in June. There was not a speck of white on her thick, luxurious fur. Charlotte wrapped her long, furry tail delicately around her feet.

As Becky reached towards her, the cat stood
up, took several steps back to the corner, and sat
down again.

"She's beautiful," Becky lamented. "Maybe, she needs
a little time."

"Right," Amy Jo said doubtfully. "Let's just feed her and
check on the freezer." As Amy Jo opened the cupboard, she
saw a note taped to a can of cat food. "What's this?"

Becky stood up and joined her friend at the cupboard.
She tore off the note and read it.

Amy Jo and Becky,

*I couldn't reach you by phone, but Charlotte will need
medication while we are gone. She became ill, so the girls
and I took her to see Dr. Ullmer on Main Street. The girls
are so upset. One of them allowed Charlotte to go outside
for overnight and she got into a terrible fight with another
cat. She developed an infection from the bites and needs to
take one-half pill twice each day. The pill bottle is on the
counter. I hope you don't mind. We'll pay you extra when
we get back.*

Thanks so much,

Mrs. Funderburg

"Oh, poor Charlotte," murmured Becky.

"Half a pill?" Amy Jo looked at the bottle, then at the
cat. "How are we supposed to do that?" she asked. "I know
we'll give her a whole pill, and she can spit half of it out."

Becky ignored her friend as she took a knife she'd
found in a drawer and cut the pill in two. Then, she
crushed the half pill with two spoons and rummaged
through a couple of cabinet doors until she located some

27

peanut butter. "Let's try this," she said as she scooped some out with the same knife. Becky placed the crushed half pill in the middle of the peanut butter and slid all of it onto the tip of her finger. She walked over to the other end of the table and got down on her hands and knees in front of Charlotte. Slowly she extended the finger with the peanut butter and pill. "Here, little Charlotte," she said in a soft, low voice.

Amy Jo folded her arms and leaned against the counter. "Little Charlotte?" she muttered to herself.

Charlotte studied Becky for a few seconds, then began to sniff at her finger. She pulled back. Intelligent green eyes studied Becky's kindly hazel ones for 30 seconds. Charlotte sniffed again and began to lick the peanut butter. Soon, the peanut butter and pill were safely inside Charlotte's stomach.

Amy Jo dumped cat food into the bowl, then positioned herself seven feet away.

Charlotte looked at both girls. She snaked through the legs of the chairs until she reached the bowl. Carefully, she began to nibble at the food.

Becky eased herself down on the floor close to Charlotte. Every few seconds, she scooted her body an inch closer.

Charlotte continued to eat the food in the bowl, but her eyes were fixed on Becky.

Becky reached ever so slowly towards the cat. She scratched gently behind Charlotte's ear and was rewarded with a soft purr.

Amy Jo watched her friend and Charlotte for a few minutes. She was impressed. "I take it back about not making friends," she said as she pushed through the swinging door. "Time to check the freezer."

Becky allowed the door to come back again, then pushed her way through it. Once on the other side, she asked. "What did you say?"

"Freezer," Amy Jo called over her shoulder. "Time to check it."

"Where is it?"

"In the basement," answered Amy Jo.

In the hallway, there was a door set in the wall that was part of the stairway. The door fit so perfectly into the paneling, that it was not apparent unless someone was looking for it.

"Wow!" Becky remarked. "I didn't see this on our way past."

"I know," Amy Jo agreed as she opened the door. "Mr. Funderburg said it was a little tricky to find."

They fumbled for the light switch and flipped it on. The light bulb at the bottom of the narrow steps didn't give off much light. Each step creaked. Nobody would ever sneak up on you down here. They popped open the door of the freezer and a blast of cold air greeted them.

Becky peered inside. "They've sure got a lot of food in here," she commented. "No wonder they want us to check it."

"Yeah," agreed Amy Jo. "Mrs. Funderburg has a garden behind the trees in the backyard. She freezes a lot of stuff."

"My Mom does that, too," said Becky.

Amy Jo shut the freezer door. "Okay, works fine, let's go," she said, leading them up the steps.

They shut the basement door and walked to the front of the hallway. Suddenly, they stopped mid-stride and looked at each other. It was undeniable. The smell of cigarette smoke hung in the air, and it hadn't been there when they first came in.

"Somebody's in this house," said Amy Jo softly.

CHAPTER 4

The Hidden Door

Becky swallowed hard. "I just knew this wasn't going to be as easy as we thought," she whispered.

Amy Jo tiptoed to the edge of the stairs and looked up. "I don't hear anything," she mouthed the words. She signaled for Becky to listen at the living room door while she placed her ear to the library door.

Their eyes stared at each other across the space of the hallway as their ears were pressed to the two doors. They shook their heads and met at the front door.

Becky's fair skin had lost all of its color. "Let's go home," she pleaded

For once Amy Jo didn't argue. "Good idea," she said, opening the door.

They hung the key back on the bug zapper pole in the backyard, then walked briskly down Center Street toward the paddock.

"Maybe we better stop by and talk to Officer Higgins," Becky suggested.

Amy Jo was silent for a few seconds. "There might be some simple reason why we smelled that," she decided. "If it happens again, we'll go talk to him about it."

The grass always looks greener somewhere else. Ginger and Oreo decided that they preferred the grass under the tree behind Hank's Ice Cream Store to what they ate in their own paddock. They eyed Amy Jo and Becky casually as the girls passed them walking toward the gate. Rarely did the girls have to call their ponies, but they called the mares now and were totally ignored. Worse yet, the mares turned their back ends to them. The ponies did not want to go home. Ginger and Oreo usually trotted over to the girls because they were glad to see them. Now, they stepped deeper into the shade of the tree.

"So, that's how it is, huh?" said Amy Jo opening the gate. "Well, I guess it's no candy for you, then," she warned.

"I know what to do," said Becky, pulling two pieces of candy from her pocket. She gave one to Amy Jo. Together they rattled the paper wrapper that held the candy.

Ginger and Oreo stopped eating and lifted their heads. Their ears cocked in the direction of the candy. Suddenly, the grass lost its pizazz, and the ponies trotted over to the gate with their ears forward. The girls held out their hands as the mares nibbled at the bribe. As they chewed, their muzzles nosed away at the girls' pockets.

Becky grabbed the bridle, eased Oreo's nose away from her pocket, and drew the reins over her pony's head. She slid the bit between the mare's teeth, then fastened the buckles in place. The saddle was placed in the middle of the wide white stripe running around the pony's middle.

Amy Jo tossed the saddle blanket onto Ginger's chestnut back. She smoothed out all the wrinkles before fitting the saddle on top of the blanket just behind Ginger's withers. She eased the tension on the front edge of the blanket so it wouldn't rub her pony's skin. Drawing the girth under her pony's belly, she tightened and buckled it so it wouldn't slip when she hoisted herself into the saddle.

The girls mounted their ponies, then reined  them to the right and headed toward Quarry Road. Amy Jo was deep in thought. Becky was trying hard not to think about anything.

Amy Jo turned into the lane leading back to their houses. Becky didn't have to rein Oreo to the right, the mare could walk from the ice cream store to the barn with her eyes closed.

"The art gallery was fun," said Becky, in an attempt to get Amy Jo's mind off the cigarette smoke. Too late, she realized that there was a mystery at the art gallery as well as the house.

Amy Jo kept her focus on the road in front of Ginger's hoofs. "Yeah, that, too," she answered.

When the girls reached the barn, they hopped off and ran up the stirrups to keep them from banging the ponies' sides. In the barn, the tack came off, halters replaced the bridles, and the ponies were fastened to crossties. Now the tricky part began. Ginger didn't like having her ears brushed, and Oreo didn't like the space between her eyes being messed with.

Amy Jo stretched to her full height in order to brush Ginger's mane. "That cat is supposed to have that medicine twice a day you know," she began.

Becky stood on a stool and combed through her pony's forelock. "I haven't forgotten," she said, grabbing hold of Oreo's halter to hold her still.

"We'll have to go back tonight to give her that second dose."

Becky's comb halted in mid-air. "Nighttime again? Oh, no . . . well, can't be helped. We have to make sure Charlotte gets her medicine."

Amy Jo tossed her brush in the corner. She unfastened the crossties and led Ginger to her stall. "We'd better give the place a look around," Amy Jo suggested as she took off the mare's halter.

Becky hopped down from the stool and faced her friend. "Oh, great," she lamented. "Why don't we give Charlotte her medicine and look around tomorrow when it's light?"

Amy Jo fastened the stall door. "Tell you what, I'll look around while you take care of the cat."

Becky lead Oreo to her stall as she thought about it. "Okay," she finally said.

Amy Jo stood with her hand on top of the stall door. "The Funderburg family doesn't smoke, so there's no chance that the smell was some kind of leftover odor. Somebody was in there. Seems like we owe it to the Funderburgs to check it out."

Becky sat on the tack truck, her face a study in misery. "I know, I know," she agreed.

Amy Jo stood in front of her friend. "I'll be done with everything I need to do at home by 7:30 or 8:00. What do you say we go over right after that while there's still plenty of daylight?"

Becky perked up. "Okay, eight o'clock's not too bad."

Amy Jo nodded her head, then headed for the door. "Okay, I'm going home now," she called over her shoulder. "I'll be back after dinner."

*   *   *   *

Ginger and Oreo eyed each other as they sauntered down Center Street. They were confused. They'd already been to the

34

ice cream store. Where were they headed now?
When the girls stopped at the Funderburg house,
the ponies' heads popped up in surprise. They'd
never been here before. The girls dismounted and led the mares
around to the back of the house towards a pole with a strange
light on top of it. Their eyes widened and their nostrils flared.
Zap! The sound it made was even scarier. Ginger and Oreo shot
backwards towards the road.

Amy Jo tightened her hold on the reins in her hand
and scurried closer to her pony's side. "It's all right,
Ginger. That old bug zapper isn't going to hurt you," she
said as she gently led the mare forward.

"Easy, Oreo," Becky soothed, patting her pony's neck.

The girls took off the bridles and replaced them with
halters, while the ponies snorted their disapproval of the
strange light. Next, the girls slipped halters over the mares'
heads and tied the end of the lead line to a branch far from
the bug zapper where the mares could graze while the girls
were in the house. They grabbed the key off the pole and
walked around to the front door.

Charlotte heard them come in and sashayed down the
hallway as only a beautiful cat who's accustomed to constant
adulation can. She stopped in front of Becky and gave the
girl permission to stroke her luxurious fur.

Becky leaned over to scratch behind her ear. "We came
back to give you another pill, you little darling."

Amy Jo rolled her eyes. "While you're giving 'little darling'
her pill, I'm going to have a look upstairs. When you get done,
do you think you could tackle the library and living room?"

Becky looked at the doors to the left. Daylight was still
streaming in through the long windows on each side of the door.
"Okay," she said as she led Charlotte to the kitchen.

Amy Jo walked upstairs to search bedrooms and bathrooms. The girls' rooms didn't turn up much beyond the usual stuff . . . dolls, stuffed toys, lots of books.

She strolled to the other end of the hallway to the master bedroom. The bed looked a little rumpled but only on one side. Amy Jo pursed her lips. One of the Funderburgs must have packed early and decided to rest . . . maybe, but people don't usually rest the morning of a long trip.

Crossing the room to the closet, Amy Jo rested her hand on the door knob for only a second. Some might consider going through the closet snooping, but detectives were supposed to snoop. "Hm," she murmured squatting down. Slippers sat beside a pair of sneakers and dress shoes. The slippers were decidedly smaller than the shoes. Amy Jo peaked inside the shoes, size 12. The slippers were a size 10, she noted, on the bottom. Strange. Maybe the Funderburgs had a smaller relative who forgot to take his slippers on the last visit. Could be that, but it was still odd.

Master bathroom was next. Nothing out of place there. As Amy Jo turned to leave, she reached inside the tub and ran her hand over the shower liner. She stopped short and stepped inside the tub. The liner was damp in a couple of places. A frown creased her brow. Could dampness linger over a two-day period? Perhaps. She looked inside the linen closest where there were two towel racks. One of the towels was slightly damp as well. The other one was completely dry. The damp one was folded differently, too. Amy Jo leaned against the wall and studied the towels. Could be that one of the Funderburgs showered the night before they left, and the other one must have showered the day of the trip . . . two days ago. Would a towel be damp after two days? She closed the door and headed for the stairway. Some things didn't quite add up, but you couldn't call in the police  over an odd pair of slippers, a damp towel and shower liner.

Downstairs, she walked from room to room looking for Becky. "Okay, I give up," she said, raising her voice. "Where are you?" Nothing. She looked out the kitchen window. There was enough daylight left that she could see the ponies grazing contentedly in the backyard. For once, they weren't having to swat insects off each other. The bug zapper was doing its job.

Amy Jo rubbed her hand over her mouth as she returned to the front hallway. "Aha, basement!" she said triumphantly. She flipped on the basement switch and scooted downstairs. It took one second to determine that Becky wasn't down there either. She returned to the hallway and just stood there. Amy Jo's mind was in an unusual state of activity; she was thinking hard but nothing was happening.

A scratching sound came from the library. Amy Jo brightened as she walked through the library door. Her face fell. It was only Charlotte scratching away at one of the bookcases. Heart racing, Amy Jo sat on a chair facing the desk and frowned. What was she going to tell Mr. and Mrs. Allison? Becky would never leave without telling her. She wasn't like that. And she certainly would take Oreo with her if she did leave.

From the bookcase, Charlotte continued to scratch away. Finally, she stopped, looked at Amy Jo, and softly meowed.

Amy Jo studied the cat. Slowly, she stood up and walked to where Charlotte was standing. She placed both hands on the bookcase. First, she pushed on each book from the top to the bottom of each shelf. She placed her hands together and pressed them to her lips while she closely eyed the end of each shelf. There was a knot in the wood just to the side of the fourth shelf. Cautiously, she reached forward and pressed against it. A catch released, and the bookcase swung inward into a secret passage.

Chapeter 5
The Black Light

"Stop!" she heard Becky scream. "Stop!"

"Where are you?" Amy Jo hollered back.

"I'm at the bottom of some steps!" Becky returned. "I'm looking for a light switch or something. But now that you've found me, I'm coming up. Whatever you do, don't let that door close or we'll both be trapped!"

Amy Jo firmly held the door open while Becky climbed the steps and joined her in the library.

Becky collapsed on one of the chairs; her face was drawn and pale. Charlotte jumped on her lap, and Becky absently stroked her fur.

The door was on a spring. As soon as Amy Jo took her hand away, it shut quickly and soundlessly.

Amy Jo stood looking from the door to Becky. "What happened?"

Becky was quiet for a full sixty seconds, then slowly came to life. "I was searching the library, just like you asked," she said, finally able to speak. "I don't know exactly how it happened, but suddenly I was on the other side of that bookcase. And it was dark. I couldn't find a light switch or a door handle to get back into the room. I tried pounding on the back of that door, but you didn't hear me. I thought maybe it might be soundproof, so I went down the steps and felt along the wall trying to find a switch. I walked a long way. I felt like I was

down there for hours, and that nobody would ever find me."
Tears were sliding down her cheeks.

Amy Jo's eyes filled with tears as she watched her friend
relive the terror of the past half hour. She stepped forward,
squatted down, and patted Becky's arm. Amy Jo and the cat
looked at each other. A silent truce was declared. Amy Jo
reached out and stroked Charlotte's fur. "Let's get the ponies
and go home," she finally said.

Becky picked up Charlotte and carried her back to the
kitchen. After checking the cat's water bowl, Becky followed
Amy Jo to the doorway. They locked up and walked to the
backyard.

As Amy Jo hung up the key, Becky drew in her breath
sharply. Amy Jo looked down as Becky extended her hands
further into the light created by the bug zapper.

"Look!" Becky said with a trembling voice. "They're
glowing!"

Amy Jo stepped closer and took hold of her hands. She
studied the palms for only a second. "They're fluorescing,"
she said with certainty.

"Fluorescing?" Becky stammered. "Is that bad?" she
asked. "Does that mean something terrible is going to happen to me?"

Amy Jo stood thinking. "No," she answered absently.
"But that means you've probably touched something that
has zinc sulfide in it."

"Zinc sulfide?!" Becky's voice echoed her state of mind.
"That doesn't sound too good," she continued. "Is it poi-
sonous?"

Amy Jo heard the panic in Becky's voice. Her friend had
been trapped in a passage and now this. "No, zinc sulfide is a
chemical. I've seen it used at museums to impress people," she

said reassuringly. "You know, you look in the display case and there's nothing there. Then they turn on the black light and these words suddenly appear. But, you can use zinc sulfide to write a secret message, too."

In her curiosity, Becky lost some of her anxiety. "How can you write a secret message with it?" she asked.

"Well," Amy Jo began. "You can mix zinc sulfide in a water solution and then paint it onto something. I suspect that in touching the walls down there, you ran into some of that stuff."

"If I'd found a light switch, I would have seen what it was," Becky said.

Amy Jo shook her head. "I doubt it."

"Why not?" asked Becky

"That's how you can use it to write secret messages," Amy Jo explained. "You need a special light to make it visible so you can see it."

Becky frowned. This whole thing was beginning to smell suspiciously like another case. "What kind of light?"

"A black light."

"A black light?" echoed Becky.

"Yeah," said Amy Jo. "Take this bug zapper. It's different from a regular light bulb. It's a black light. That's why we didn't see your 'glowing hands' in the house under the regular lights, but we see it under this bug zapper light."

Becky stared at Amy Jo. Her head was spinning. "Can't we just forget about this? I don't want to get stuck down there investigating it. Or better yet . . . we could go to Officer Higgins and tell him," she added hopefully.

Amy Jo's face was as sober as it ever got. "Let's get the ponies," she said as she stepped across the lawn.

Moments earlier, Ginger and Oreo neighed softly as the girls came around the corner of the house. When the girls fell to discussing zinc sulfide, the ponies lowered their heads and grazed a little longer. Now that Amy Jo and Becky headed towards them, the mares took a step forward, eager to return to their stalls. They didn't balk at having the bits placed in their mouths or their girths tightened. They wanted a long drink of water. If they were lucky . . . one or two carrots.

The girls walked their ponies out to Center Street. There was a decorative rock close by, and it was easier to mount the mares from the rock.

Amy Jo broke the silence. "You see, it wouldn't be any good going to Officer Higgins."

Becky's anxiety rose. "Why not?"

"He'd say something like, 'There's no law against having a secret passage under your house.'"

Becky thought a moment. "I know," she finally said.

Amy Jo turned to her partner. "And besides that, we don't know what the message says yet. Maybe it was written years ago or maybe it was just a game some kids played." Amy Jo continued, "The problem is you've had a terrible scare. Tomorrow you'll feel a lot better about everything."

To the bottom of her toenails, Becky highly doubted this. Changing the subject, she asked. "I guess you know all about this zinc sulfide and black light business because of your Dad?"

"Yeah," said Amy Jo. "We used to work together in the basement before he died. That's where the lab is," she explained. "He'd come home from the police department stumped about a tough case, and we'd go down and work on it together. Of course, he never told me any secret stuff or anything. He just explained how different things worked in our lab."

"Do you have any of this zinc sulfide down  there?" Becky asked.

"Yeah, and better yet," she added with a certain pride. "I have a black light."

Becky reached forward to smooth out Oreo's mane. She patted her on the neck and settled back in her saddle. "I don't know, Amy Jo," she said, guessing where the black light would lead them.

Amy Jo felt her saddle slipping. She moved her left leg forward and raised the flap on the saddle.

Ginger turned her head around as soon as she felt Amy Jo's leg on her neck. She knew what was coming and shook her head. The girth around her stomach was about to get tighter.

"Just a notch, Ginger," said Amy Jo soothingly as she gently pulled the straps.

The girls continued in silence until they turned off Quarry Road into the lane.

Amy Jo looked over at her friend. "I know you don't want to think about it, Beck, but we'll make absolutely sure that we have that door blocked open before we go down there."

Becky was a study in conflict. "I know you think that's what will happen, and that we'll be safe, but . . ."

Amy Jo thought for a moment. "Okay, how about if we don't go down there until we've figured out how to open the door from the other side of the bookcase?"

Becky sighed and looked at the ground in front of Oreo's feet. "I don't know," she said softly.

"Look, one of us will stay on the library side of the room, while the other one looks for the handle on the other side. That way we can't get trapped. I mean, we'll still block it open, but just in case something happens we'll know where the handle is." She waited until they got to the barn and then asked. "What do you say?"

Becky dismounted and flipped the left stirrup over the saddle so that she could loosen Oreo's girth. "I don't know, Amy Jo," she repeated.

Amy Jo pressed on. "Okay, here's what we'll do," she said in a rush. "Tomorrow you come down to my house first thing. We'll dig around for the black light and make sure it still works. We'd better take a couple of regular flashlights, too. Then, we'll come back here and get the ponies." She chanced a peek at her partner to see how she was taking all this. *Not too good* she thought. Then, with sudden inspiration. "Got to feed Charlotte and give her the medicine, don't forget."

Becky lifted her head and looked at Amy Jo. "Oh, yeah, I forgot. She's got to have that twice a day."

They walked the ponies into the barn and flipped on the switch. Both ponies tried to walk into their stalls with all their tack still on. The girls firmly pushed them to the crossties where they exchanged bridles for halters. Nine o'clock was no time for a thorough brush down. So, they wiped the saddle area and face where the bridle had made the mares sweat, then lead them to their stalls. Two carrots were broken up and tossed in each pony's feed bucket . . . their reward for not complaining.

Amy Jo walked Becky across the stone driveway to the back door of her white, two-storied house. "You okay?" she asked.

Becky nodded. "Thanks," she answered.

"Okay," she said. "Then, I'll see you at my house at 8:30 tomorrow morning." And with that, Amy Jo wheeled around, got on her bike, and pedaled home.

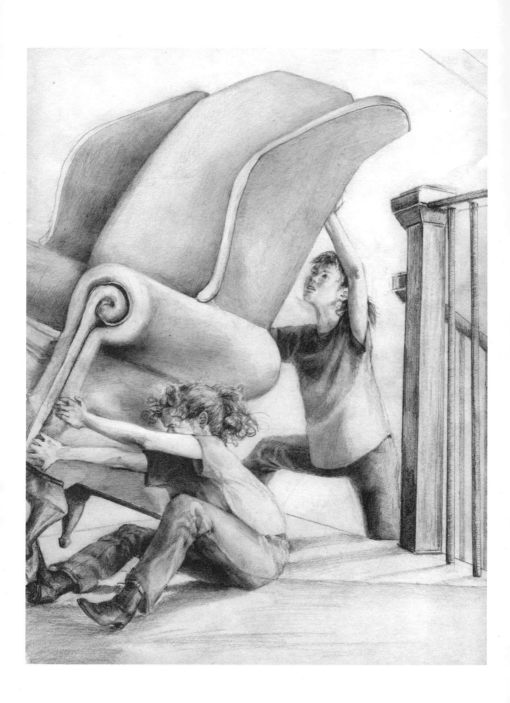

CHAPTER 6

Something to Hide

Next morning Becky knocked at the kitchen door to the Ryan home.

Mrs. Ryan answered the door. She wore a long, blue bathrobe and balanced a cup of coffee in a saucer in her hand. Even at 8:30 in the morning, she was lovely. She had Amy Jo's auburn hair and blue eyes, but somehow, on Elizabeth Ryan, they looked elegant. Perhaps there was a shred of hope for Amy Jo down the road.

"Why, hello, Becky." Mrs. Ryan always seemed genuinely happy to see her daughter's friend. "Would you like a little breakfast while Amy Jo finishes hers?" she asked.

Amy Jo picked up her cereal bowl as she rose from the table. "I'm finished, Mom." She hung over the bowl and ate the last two bites on her way to the sink.

Becky returned Mrs. Ryan's smile. "I've already eaten, Mrs. Ryan. Thanks anyway."

"Come on, Beck," Amy Jo said, leading the way to the basement.

"I'll be leaving for work soon, Amy Jo," called Mrs. Ryan at the top of the basement steps. "I'll be back around noon."

"Okay, Mom. See you then," Amy Jo called over her shoulder.

"Goodbye, Mrs. Ryan," said Becky.

"Goodbye, Becky," Mrs. Ryan returned. She shook her head as she looked at the cereal bowl in the sink. Meals were always a race.

Amy Jo moved two boxes away from the corner, then opened a third box. "Aha, here it is," she said triumphantly. "Now, let's see," she continued absently as she took something that looked like a flashlight out of a box. She placed the black light on a long, wide table which had stools tucked under its ledge.

Amy Jo strolled over to the far wall where bottles were lined up on two shelves. She walked along the shelves murmuring incomprehensible names on the labels until she stopped. "Okay, here it is," she said, pulling down a bottle. "Yep, zinc sulfide. That'll do it." She mixed some of the zinc sulfide into a pan of water. Then, she dipped a paint brush into the solution and painted a narrow strip down the palm of her hand. "Flip the light off over there, will you, Beck?" she asked.

Becky walked over to the light switch and turned it to the "off" position. Once it was completely dark, Amy Jo flipped on the black light and pointed it at her hand. "It's fluorescing!" There was excitement in Becky's voice.

Amy Jo smiled. "Right!" she said. "Looks just like your hand did last night."

Becky nodded her head. "Yeah, I get it now," she said with a relaxed voice, then turned on the light. "I'm not worried about it anymore."

"Good, I knew you wouldn't be," said Amy Jo as she picked up two regular flashlights. She gave them both to her partner and carefully placed the black light in a small cushioned bag, then put the bag into her backpack. "Okay, let's get the ponies and go to the Funderburg's," she said, placing her arms through the straps of the backpack.

An hour later, their chores were done, the mares were grazing in Hank's paddock, and the girls were in front of the bookcase.

Becky's brow creased deeply. The assurance generated in Amy Jo's basement had disappeared. She wasn't the tiniest bit curious about fluorescing material or anything else. She just did not want to get stuck down in that secret passage again.

Amy Jo pressed the release and the door swung in. The interior looked like the inside of a black hole at midnight. Amy Jo swallowed hard as she stepped across the threshold. She turned to Becky. "Now, you saw the place where you have to push to open the door, didn't you?"

"Yes," Becky tapped on the knot in the wood.

"Good," Amy Jo replied. She stood and thought some more. "Now, remember it's probably soundproof on the other side, so even if you don't hear me pound on the door, just open it in a couple of minutes anyway. You got that?" she continued, studying her friend's face carefully to make sure there was no misunderstanding.

Becky nodded her head. "Gotcha," she said as her eyes checked the telephone setting on the desk . . . just in case. "I'll give you a couple of minutes, then open the door," she repeated.

Amy Jo nodded her head in return. She flipped on the flashlight and closed the door. First, she scanned the walls with her flashlight looking for a light switch. Nothing. The back of the door seemed fairly tight to the wall. No light came through at all. Amy Jo stood close to the door with the light beam from her flashlight directly in front of her. She lifted her arm and allowed the light to pass all along the seam of the door until she had covered all four edges. It was relatively cool in there, but a tiny trickle of sweat slid down her back anyway. Amy Jo allowed her fingers to brush across the wood starting at the top. One quarter of the way down, she felt something. It was like a metal ring that fit level with the wood. She slid her finger into it and pulled. The door opened. She stepped back to allow the door to swing towards her and walked into the library.

Becky closed her eyes with relief and sat down.

Amy Jo sat across from her and wiped her forehead on the sleeve of her shirt. "Went pretty well," she commented with more confidence than she actually felt. "It didn't take long to find it."

Becky looked up. "It seemed like you were gone forever."

"Okay," said Amy Jo as she stood up. "Let's just block the door with this chair and we'll be home free."

Becky picked up the flashlights. "Here it comes," she whimpered under her breath.

The girls lifted the chair next to the desk, but neither of them were satisfied that it was heavy enough to block the door adequately.

They scoured the entire house until they found a chair on the second floor that the two of them together could barely budge. They lifted the four-legged giant and manhandled the monster down the steps and around the corner. Only two scrapes on the hardwood floor stood between them and complete success. One of them was deep enough to nudge their conscience. They'd have some explaining to do, but it couldn't be helped. They jammed the chair in the door's opening, with positively no room to pass by it. Crawling over the seat with their backpacks, the girls stood on the other side of the chair with more assurance that the door couldn't possibly close on this monstrosity.

Cautiously, they eased down the steps. Unbelievably, every few steps, Becky would turn around to make sure the chair was holding the door open. Her hand trailed along the wall to steady her descent.

As the girls reached the bottom of the steps, Amy Jo aimed the black light at the stairwell walls. There were dashes of lines running about three feet off the floor of the tunnel. The passage did not just begin at the bottom of the steps, a tunnel ran both ways as far as their flashlights could reach turning the light to the left and then to the right. They decided to turn left. That was the direction that would lead them towards the heart of Bedford. Once they rounded the corner at the bottom of the steps, it was completely dark outside the ring of light created by each flashlight.

When Amy Jo aimed the black light at Becky's hand, it was once again fluorescing. "See," she said, nodding at the lines on the wall which were invisible a second ago. "That's what you've been touching."

Becky cast another anxious look over her shoulder. "Now what?" she asked.

Amy Jo stepped into the center of the tunnel and looked both ways. "These lines must be here to tell someone which way to go," she finally said. "I suspect that passages lead off the main tunnel. So, somebody put the lines here to know which passage to take and how to get back without getting lost."

Curiosity drew Becky to Amy Jo's side. "But, why would anyone want to go from one place to another down here?" she asked. "Why go to all the trouble of coming down here when it's easier to move around above ground?"

"The usual reason," said Amy Jo turning left.

Casting a last look over her shoulder at the propped door, Becky followed Amy Jo. "What's the usual reason?" she asked.

"Something to hide," said Amy Jo as she kept the black light steady on the lines.

"Something to hide," echoed Becky. "What's there to hide?"

"That's what we're going to find out," explained Amy Jo.

"Oh, swell," Becky began. "What if I don't want to find out anything. I just know we're going to round the corner and come face to face with somebody I don't want to meet. Or the door leading down here will shut and somehow it'll lock. We'll spend the rest of our lives as cave people or something. What am I saying . . . we'll die of starvation before we can officially become cave people."

Amy Jo tripped and steadied herself against the tunnel wall with her left hand. "Easy Beck, don't get rattled. We're just getting started."

"Yeah, that's what worries me. We're just getting started."

Amy Jo reached behind and drew Becky to her side. "Keep your flashlight aimed ahead of us while I keep the black light focused on the wall," she directed. "I don't want to trip again."

Becky looked down at the floor of the tunnel. "It's not too even in here, is it?" she noted, then thought for a moment. "I hope we never have to run away from someone down here."

CHAPTER 7

Too Many Tunnels

The girls walked through an endless succession of passages. They zigzagged twists and turns that lead them farther away from the main trunk of the passageway. The dashes of lines became dots of zinc sulfide reminiscent of a map telling them where to go. Without the dots, they'd be totally lost.

The bobbing circle of light surrounding Becky's flashlight had an unnerving effect. "You know this reminds me of Hansel and Gretel," she began shakily.

Amy Jo took her eyes off the dots long enough to look incredulously at her partner. "Hansel and Gretel?" she exclaimed. "That's a stretch."

"Not really," Becky countered. "Now, look at it this way," she raced on nervously. "Hansel and Gretel were lost in the woods, and the only way they could find their way back was because they had dropped pieces of bread along the way," she explained. "So, these dots on the wall are like the pieces of bread."

Amy Jo raised an eyebrow. "Well, don't forget that the wicked witch put Hansel in a cage so she could fatten him up for dinner," she reminded her friend. "So you'd better hope there's nobody down here who hasn't eaten for a while."

Becky caught her breath. "Oh, I forgot about that part."

Amy Jo walked solidly on, but an idea invaded her mind,

and she became increasingly uneasy. "We'll be in a pickle if that happens," she muttered. Her concerns cranked a little tighter, but she hadn't realized that the last few words of her thoughts were said aloud.

Becky turned to her friend. "What's that supposed to mean?" she asked anxiously.

To avoid frightening her partner, Amy Jo deliberately mumbled something vague about being hungry for lunch hoping that Becky would let go of it . . . Becky didn't.

"What? I still can't hear you!" said Becky, grabbing Amy Jo's arm.

"I said I was just thinking about lunch!" Amy Jo said louder.

"You expect me to believe that you were talking about lunch?" Becky was offended.

"What's the matter?" Amy Jo avoided the issue. "You got something against pickles?"

"Give me a break," Becky continued. "You're worried about something, and I want to know what it is."

The black light in Amy Jo's hand flickered. "Well, it's just that . . . I haven't used this black light for a while, and I don't know how good the batteries are."

Silence fell, but Amy Jo could feel the pressure rising.

"You mean to tell me, that the only thing that stands between us and becoming cavegirls is that black light, and you don't know how much longer the batteries are going to last?" She said it quietly, but the impact of her words were immense.

Amy Jo stopped and faced her partner. "You're right," she said. "Let's go back."

With each step and juncture of passages, the significance of not knowing which passage to take without the black light sunk in.

"I am so stupid," muttered Amy Jo.

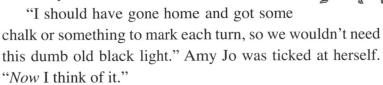

"Why?"

"I should have gone home and got some chalk or something to mark each turn, so we wouldn't need this dumb old black light." Amy Jo was ticked at herself. "*Now* I think of it."

"If we get out of this alive," Becky began, "we'd better sit down and think of everything we need before we come back here again."

Amy Jo smiled in spite of herself. "You mean you're willing to come down here again?"

"I can't believe I said that," countered Becky quickly. "Maybe, but maybe not." She thought for a moment longer. "That is if the chair hasn't slipped so that the door's locked when we get back." She definitely felt negative about the entire situation.

The black light flickered again just as they came to a juncture where three passages branched off. This time it didn't come back on.

Becky swallowed hard. She stared at the walls of the three passages willing the dots to come alive.

Amy Jo tapped the side of the black light with the palm of her hand. She didn't know if it would help, but she'd seen plenty of people bang on soda machines and pay phones and sometimes it worked. Anyway, she figured it wouldn't hurt.

The girls stepped into the middle of the juncture shining the flashlights down each of the three passages. The tunnel gave them three choices. Only one of the three would lead them back to the stairs. The other two could lead them anywhere. The walls seemed to close in around them. It was deathly still except for the punctuated breathing of both girls.

Amy Jo looked sideways at Becky. "It could be worse," she commented.

"It could be worse?" said Becky as she faced her partner. "We have no idea where to go, and you say it could be worse?" Fear of the unknown forced her to ask. "Okay, tell me what could be worse than spending what is left of my very short life down in these tunnels?"

Amy Jo shrugged her shoulders trying to make light of it. "The batteries on the two regular flashlights could go out."

Becky was aghast. "How old are those batteries?" she asked, but was afraid of the answer.

Amy Jo took her time in answering. "Couldn't say," she finally said. "Been around a while, I know that."

Becky leaned against the cave wall. "I changed my mind," she decided. "If we ever get out of this alive, I am never, as in never ever, coming down here again."

In frustration Amy Jo whacked the side of the black light again. This time it came on. The dots sprang out on the second passage to the right. "Let's go!" she nearly shouted, and they leaped forward as fast as the uneven floor would allow.

Two more passages and it began to look familiar. The dots became strings of lines as they had first appeared at the bottom of the steps.

"I think this is the last passage," Amy Jo commented as they rounded a corner.

Becky sighed with relief. "I hope so."

As they walked up the steps which led to the library, they saw Charlotte curled up on the chair which held the door open.

Becky picked up the cat and sat heavily on one of the chairs.

Amy Jo dragged the chair away from the opening and sat opposite her friend. "Okay," she began, "I've been thinking about what we'll need."

Charlotte began to purr as Becky stroked her fur. "You can tell me all about it when you get back, because I'm staying right here."

Amy Jo ignored Becky's comment and continued on. "We'll need some chalk, extra batteries, and a compass," she said with finality.

Becky allowed her hand to slip off the cat's head. She leaned back in her chair and looked up at the ceiling.

"The compass is going to save us a lot of time," Amy Jo continued. "We won't get lost."

Charlotte nudged Becky's hand. Becky sat up again and resumed petting the cat's head. "Okay." She took the bait. "Chalk and batteries I get, but why a compass?"

Amy Jo smiled at the other girl. "Can't you see, Beck?" she explained. "These dots are leading somebody to some specific place. It would be useful to know where we are going when we're down there."

"But I don't get it," Becky protested. "How will a compass help us?"

Amy Jo scrunched up her lips and thought of how to explain it. "Well, I thought if we'd stand in the Funderburg's backyard and face different buildings in the village, we could point the compass towards each building and see what the reading is. Say we're facing Hank's Ice Cream Shop and we point the compass towards it. Well, Hank's shop is directly north which is zero degrees. So, if we're walking down a passage and the compass needle is pointing at zero, we know we're heading towards Hank's shop. Get it?"

Becky's face had regained some of its color. "Yes, I get it," she answered. "That means if we turn around and the compass reads one hundred eighty degrees, we know that we're going towards our lane off Quarry Road, which is south."

Amy Jo sat up and leaned forwards. "Right! Now, we need paper and pencil to write down the main buildings and their readings from the compass, so that when we're in the tunnels we'll know where we're headed."

Becky looked at her friend in admiration. "That's brilliant," she said softly.

Amy Jo lifted her eyebrows and thought for a second. "Yeah, that's pretty much brilliant," she said, then continued. "One thing's for sure, we need to measure the degrees for the art gallery since that might have something to do with the case."

"You're right there, too," Becky agreed.

Amy Jo relaxed a bit. Everything seemed to be back on track. "Okay, we'll bring what we need back tonight when we give Charlotte her second medication." She had been calling the cat by her given name ever since "her majesty" had saved Becky's life.

Becky stood up with Charlotte and headed for the kitchen. "Oh, no we won't," she said determinedly.

Amy Jo followed her into the hallway. "Why not?" she asked.

Without breaking stride, Becky answered over her shoulder. "It's dark at night." And she went through the kitchen's swinging door.

"Dark?" asked Amy Jo waiting for the door to swing back to her. "It's just as dark down there in the daylight as it is at night," she reasoned, slipping through on the door's next pass.

"Oh, no it's not." Becky came back.

Amy Jo cocked her head. "How do you figure?"

Becky put the cat on her little bed and stated emphatically. "It feels darker in my head, that's how I figure."

"Well, that certainly makes sense," Amy Jo said sarcastically.

"I don't care if it makes sense or not, we're not going down there until tomorrow. Anyway," said Becky with sudden inspiration, "I thought we were going to check out that airplane business that Devon was talking about."

Amy Jo took the front door key out of her pocket. "Oh, yeah, I forgot. I've got some stuff to do for Mom this afternoon," she said heading for the door. "How about if we go right after dinner tonight while there's still plenty of daylight."

The girls replaced the key on the bug zapper and walked down Quarry Road towards the paddock. This time the ponies were waiting at the gate with their heads hanging over the top board. As the girls neared, the mares bobbed their heads.

Ginger had started tapping the bottom board on the fence with her hoof when she grew impatient waiting for her treat. She tapped it now.

Amy Jo gave Becky a look that said *I've got to put a stop to this behavior.* "If she breaks that bottom board, Hank might not let us use the paddock anymore." Amy Jo opened the gate, took Ginger by the halter, and backed her up a few paces, then with a firm voice, said, "No!"

Ginger hung her head and seemed to heave a sigh. There was no sign of candy as the ponies got tacked up and led out of the paddock. Halfway down Center Street, Ginger turned her head around to look at Amy Jo.

Amy Jo leaned over and patted her pony on the neck. "I still love you," she said.

*　　*　　*　　*

The sun was casting long shadows ahead of them as the girls headed out of town on Quarry Road. Within a few minutes, they sighted the three silos off to the left.

Amy Jo stretched up in her stirrups and looked ahead. "Didn't Devon say she spotted the airplane just past the silos?" she asked her partner.

"Yes," said Becky, stretching up in her saddle and arching her neck. "I think she said it was past the silos and back off the road to the left."

"Great landmark from an airplane," said Amy Jo, surveying the height of the silos. She allowed her eyes to wander across acres of rolling pasture. "It's not very flat," she began. "Let's ride through here for a while and see if we can find a spot level enough for a plane to land."

Becky reined Oreo to the left as she followed Amy Jo and Ginger into the grass. "It was dark when Devon was here," she reminded the other girl. "Maybe she forgot exactly where she saw it."

"Maybe," said Amy Jo over her shoulder.

They rode on for a few minutes, then Amy Jo turned to her partner. "Let's split up a little bit," she said. "The search will go faster."

Becky looked to the right side of the pasture. "I'll go this way," she said. "But I won't get so far that if I holler you can't hear me."

"Okay," said Amy Jo shifting her pony  in the opposite direction.

The girls alternately scanned the horizon searching for a level spot and checked the ground directly in front of them looking for clues.

Suddenly, Becky came over the rise of a hill. She pulled up her pony sharply and cupped her hands around her mouth. "Amy Jo!" she called. "Over here!"

Chapter 8

The Unseeable

Before Becky's eyes lay the perfectly level strip of land they had been seeking. She looked into the distance and saw that Amy Jo hadn't heard her. She trotted a hundred feet in her friend's direction and called again.

Amy Jo looked up and waved her arm, then tightened her legs around Ginger and nudged the mare into a canter. Within one minute, she was standing beside Becky and Oreo.

Both girls studied the possible site of the landing strip as their ponies swatted flies off the area just behind their girths.

"Look at those bushes," said Amy Jo sweeping her arm to the right. "It's the nearest hiding place to the road. Maybe that's where Devon stood when she saw the plane."

Becky followed her partner's gaze. "They're tall enough that they could have hidden Devon and her bike," she agreed.

The girls guided their ponies toward the spot and dismounted. Bridles were replaced with halters and lead lines. Seconds later, Amy Jo and Becky tied the lead lines to bushes with lush grass surrounding them.

Side by side the girls walked into the middle of the strip. The possible landing site was about three hundred yards long and eighty feet wide. Trees and clumps of brush were located at intervals along the strip.

Amy Jo turned slowly around in a circle. "Great hiding place," she noted with surprise. "I never knew this was here."

"Neither did I," Becky agreed.

"Yeah, but you've only lived here since the beginning of summer," Amy Jo reminded her friend. "I've lived in Bedford all my life."

Becky walked the width of the strip. "Seems like the plane would have crossed here, but I don't see any tire marks," she commented.

Amy Jo shrugged her shoulders as she set off in a different direction. "Maybe the grass popped back up again. Why don't you cover that part," she suggested. "Call me if you find anything."

"Right," called Becky over her shoulder.

Amy Jo focused her eyes a few yards ahead of her feet as she walked along. She was about to turn around and head back, when her foot crunched as she stepped on something. Kneeling down, she carefully parted the grass. Now it was her turn to yell. "Beck!" she shouted. "Over here!"

Becky trotted the length of the strip and leaned over her friend's back. "What is it?" she asked.

Amy Jo carefully picked up several pieces of the broken material and laid them in the palm of her hand. She stood up and extended the pieces to Becky. "It's thin slivers of glass," she said.

Becky looked at the glass, then raised her eyes to meet Amy Jo. "What do you think it means?"

Amy Jo let her breath out slowly and thought a moment. Remembering Devon's description of the makeshift runway, she offered a suggestion. "Might be one of the light bulbs that lit the way for the pilot to land."

Becky took it a step further. "Maybe there's more."

"You're right," Amy Jo agreed. "Let's stick close together and check the ground some more."

Both girls walked in a slightly bent fashion  as they searched the ground for more glass. Soon, there was the sound of more crunching. This time it was under Becky's feet, but Amy Jo heard it, too. Both girls dropped to their knees and parted the grass.

"Here it is," said Becky as she used her thumb and fore-finger to pick up the glass.

Amy Jo stood up and drew an imaginary line between the first place they found glass and where they stood now. It's a straight line down the strip," she noted.

"Just like Devon said," added Becky.

"Yeah," said Amy Jo absently as she stood and thought.

Becky allowed her friend a moment, then asked, "What are you thinking about?"

"Well, I still can't figure out why anyone would want to land here," she began. "I mean, what are they bringing in on that plane that is so special that somebody needs to hide it as soon as it arrives. Wherever they're coming from must be too far to deliver it by car, so they have to use a plane. And why not land at the airport which is only a few miles down the road?"

Becky sighed and scratched her head. "I don't have a clue about any of this," she finally said.

Amy Jo looked along the edge of the strip. "Look, why don't we walk along the sides of the strip and see if we can find anything else. Maybe whoever it is got careless and dropped something."

Becky looked at her watch. Only one hour of sunlight left. "Okay, for a little while," she said, crossing to the far side. "I'll look over here."

"Fine," said Amy Jo making her way to the right.

The girls studied the bushes and low-hanging trees

occasionally dropping to their knees to study something up close. They were too far away from the edges of the strip to crunch on anymore glass.

As Becky neared the end of her side of the strip, she crossed the grass and joined Amy Jo. "Nothing," was all she said.

Amy Jo was sitting on the ground beside a clump of jagged bushes. She appeared totally unaware that Becky had approached.

Becky scanned the horizon, the sun had just dipped below it. "Did you hear what I said?" she asked, raising her voice.

Amy Jo looked up. It took a few seconds for her eyes to focus on her partner. She frowned slightly. "Did you say something?" she asked vaguely.

Becky spread her arms apart. "I finished my side. Didn't find anything. Nothing's here. Time to go home."

Amy Jo opened her hand and looked at a brown scrap of torn paper she'd been studying before Becky walked up. "I found something," she said in a distant voice.

Curiosity overcame Becky's desire to leave. She sat down beside her friend and leaned her head over the scrap of paper. "It just has some numbers written on it," she decided after a moment. "Is it a code or something?"

"I don't know. It depends on what was written on the rest of the paper," Amy Jo decided. "I doubt if this was left for someone else to pick up. It was probably ripped off a larger sheet of paper by accident."

Becky's face grew thoughtful. "Numbers," she finally said, then leaned over Amy Jo's hand again and nodded her head as she counted how many digits were in the code. "Eight," she decided. "That might be important."

Amy Jo looked up at her. "Eight?" she mumbled. "What's important about eight?"

Becky pressed. "When you think of numbers what do you think of?"

"Huh . . . math class!" snorted Amy Jo.

Becky sighed. "How about a bank?"

Amy Jo instantly sobered up. "The bank? What makes you think of the bank?"

"Well, my dad works at the bank, you know. And sometimes when Mom and I are waiting for him, I lean on top of one of the tellers' counters and look at the dollar bills. The Treasury Department uses eight digits to identify each bill."

Amy Jo took this in and then said, "I wonder if one of those tunnels leads to the bank?"

Becky's face sobered as well. "It's a long way underground from the Funderburg's house to the bank."

Amy Jo stood up. "It's time to go," she decided. "We need to give Charlotte her pill. I'd like to take those compass readings in the back of the Funderburg's yard so that we see which passage leads to the bank, but it's getting too dark to see the readings"

"Right," Becky readily agreed.

The girls were about halfway to the ponies when they first heard it. Someone coughed. Instinctively, they turned around, but no one was there. The wind was still, and sound carried in the pasture. The coughing stopped and the wheezing began. Fear gripped the girls as their eyes continued to search the area. They backed up, fearful of turning away from the unseeable. When they reached the mares, they turned around, lifted the skirt of the saddle to tighten the girths, and mounted from the ground. They didn't take

71

time to put the bridles back on. This time of night the ponies didn't need to be guided, they were ready to go home. Legs gripped hard, and the mares leaped into an immediate canter.

As they reached Quarry Road, they sat deeply into their saddles, pulled back on the halters, and said, "Whoa." The ponies came to a stop. The girls slid down to the ground, reached into their saddle bags, and exchanged halters and lead lines for bridles.

"I wonder if that's the same man Devon talked about yesterday?" Becky asked, fastening the buckles.

Amy Jo slipped her foot into the stirrup and swung her right leg over the saddle. "We'll ask her tomorrow when we stop for ice cream," she decided.

Further down the road Amy Jo turned to Becky. "Anyway, it had to be the same person we heard in the art gallery."

Becky nodded her head. "Had to be him," she agreed. "But why couldn't we see him, where was he?"

"And what was Cough doing in the art gallery?" Amy Jo added.

"And what's Cough doing out here now?" asked Becky, picking up on Amy Jo's nickname for the unknown man in the pasture.

They ambled on as both girls thought.

Finally, Amy Jo turned to her friend. "Maybe the tunnel goes out to the pasture. Maybe he was just inside the tunnel, which means we could hear Cough but not see him."

Becky closed her eyes and tried to calm her mounting fear. Finally, she turned a worried face to her partner. "I hope you aren't thinking about looking for the passage to the pasture."

Amy Jo didn't answer right away. "I'm not sure where to start," she admitted. "But one thing's for sure, if Cough was there the whole time, he heard every word we said."

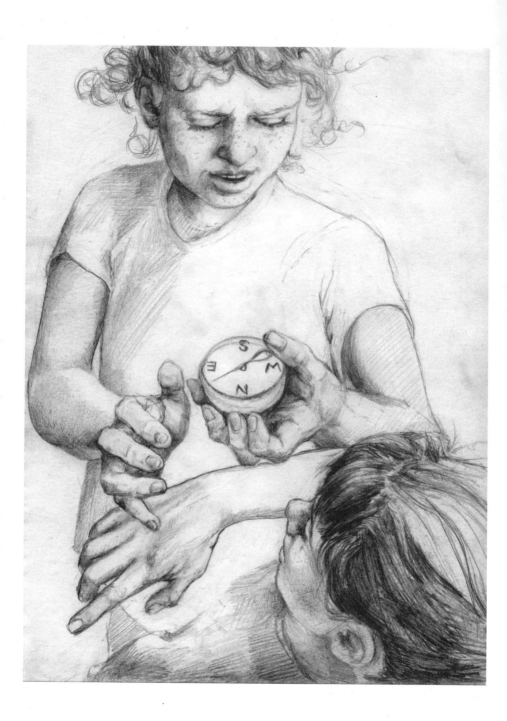

Something's Happened

Cough watched the girls canter towards the road. He ran his rough hand over his mouth and studied the skies. A clear night meant a safer landing. With shaking hands, he laid the strips of lights parallel to each other and connected it to the portable generator. Minutes later, he heard a plane flying low and heading in his direction. His throat felt tighter than usual as he flipped the switch. The double row of lights flooded the makeshift runway.

Hunter hopped down from the plane and dug the single package out of the compartment.

For the first time, Cough didn't turn off the landing lights as he approached the plane.

Hunter handed the package to Cough but kept his head down. He turned his back waiting for the package to be slit open and inspected. Instead, the unthinkable occurred. Cough spoke.

Cough's voice was raspier than usual. "Something's happened."

Hunter turned around and stared. Now, if called upon, Hunter could identify this man. "What do you mean?" was all he asked.

Cough distrusted others out of habit and experience, so the next words came uneasily to his lips. "Two girls found the door leading to the underground tunnels."

Hunter frowned. "Door leading underground?" He had no idea what was going on and was afraid he was about to find out.

At that moment, Cough wanted to take the package, give Hunter the money, and head for the tunnel entrance. But he knew that the margin of safety had already been crossed. It was too late to be careful. "I can't explain everything, but this whole operation is worth a lot of money, and these two girls are just about ready to bust the whole thing wide open."

Hunter was curious now. "How can two girls ruin everything?"

"There are a series of connecting tunnels underneath this village, and the girls were down there yesterday," Cough began. "I followed them . . . but they were making so much noise on their own that they didn't hear me." His breath came in gasps even though he was standing perfectly still. "They're going down there again . . . and this time . . . they'll find the tunnel to the art gallery."

Hunter's face paled. "What are you getting at?"

Cough looked directly into Hunter's gray eyes measuring the level he could be trusted. He flinched. Once again there was no choice. "I can't let those girls destroy a year's worth of work. I'm going to follow them . . . down there tomorrow from the Funderburg's house, and if I see that they get too close to the art gallery tunnel . . . well, I'll get them and double back through the tunnel . . . to this pasture. That's where . . . you come in."

Hunter hesitated, but he had to know where this was headed. "What do you expect me to do?" he asked.

76

"I need you to fly in here tomorrow night  before it's too dark to see the ground, because I won't be here to lay the lights out for you. Then, I'll need you to block the girls' exit out of the tunnel using the art gallery entrance." Cough spent another minute explaining how to gain access to the tunnel using the art gallery. When the pilot didn't respond, he continued. "So, you'll be in front of them, and I'll be behind them. They can't escape. We'll carry the girls through the length of the tunnel until we get to this spot, then we'll load them on the plane and take off." There, he'd said it. Now, would the pilot agree to do it. "Extra money in it for you, of course."

There it was again. Money. Hunter drew in his lips and looked at the ground. With enough money, he could pay off his debts and start over. He felt as though he'd been given one more chance at life, but he needed to ask another question. "What do you intend to do with these girls?"

Cough looked away for a moment, then turned back. "It depends on how much they find out," he finally answered. "It may be we'll just hide them away . . . for a day or two, then let them go after I've made the switch. We'll have to hide our faces, of course. We can't let them identify us."

"How big are these girls?" asked Hunter, wondering how much of a fight they might have. "About how old do you think they are?"

"Eleven or twelve, I'd say."

Hunter nodded and looked across the rolling pasture. Same age as his son.

*   *   *   *

By five p.m., Devon was elbow deep in soap suds as the girls filed into Hank's Ice Cream Shop late the following afternoon. After wiping her hands on a cloth, Devon adjusted her apron, and approached the counter. "Same as yesterday?" she inquired.

"Same as usual," Becky replied.

Amy Jo nodded. "Me, too."

Devon pointed the ice cream scooper at Amy Jo. "Chocolate chip cookie dough, right?"

"Right."

Turning to Becky, Devon continued. "Fudge ripple?"

"Fudge ripple," Becky confirmed.

Devon sighed. "I'm learning," she stated as she grabbed two ice cream glasses.

Amy Jo cleared her throat. "Becky and I went out to that spot beyond the silos last night," she said as matter-of-factly as she could.

Devon stopped dipping for a second and looked up. "You did?" she asked. "Find anything?"

Becky picked up her spoon as Devon set her ice cream on the counter. "We found some slivers of glass."

"Slivers of glass?" Devon asked.

Amy Jo dug her spoon into the chocolate chip cookie dough. "Yeah, we're thinking that they might be pieces of the string of lights you were talking about."

Devon pursed her lips. "Makes sense," she said casually, but she was relieved to hear that there was confirmation for what had happened.

"Do you remember anything else about that night?" pressed Amy Jo.

Devon frowned. "Like what?"

"Anything you might have *heard*?" Becky asked helpfully.

Devon folded her arms and thought. "Well,
I was too far away to hear them if they were
talking," she stared out the window as she continued to think. "Only thing I can think of is that one of the
men coughed a lot."

The girls stopped eating and stared at the other girl.

Amy Jo put down her spoon. "Like he had a cold or
something?"

"Not exactly," Devon decided. "It was more like one of
those raspy-type coughs that makes you think of someone
whose got a problem in his chest. You know what I
mean?"

"Yep," both girls said at the same time.

Amy Jo and Becky sat back as they swallowed the last
bite of ice cream.

Devon took that as her cue to dip up ice cream for Ginger and Oreo.

After stopping at the paddock to feed the ponies their
cones, Amy Jo and Becky walked to the backyard of the
Funderburg house.

Amy Jo double-checked the backpack for the compass,
paper, pencil and chalk. "Here, I'll measure with the compass, and you copy down the readings okay, Beck?"

Becky took the paper and pencil from her partner and sat
down on the grass. She looked up and shielded her eyes from
the sun as Amy Jo lined up the compass to the first building.

Amy Jo turned in the direction of Main Street. "Now,
let's look at it this way," she began. "Zero degrees is directly north of us, which goes right through Hank's Ice
Cream Store." Shifting a bit she added, "There's Ruthie's
Café right across the street and the art gallery next door to
that. Now, Ruthie's Café isn't a big deal, I don't think, but

the art gallery is another story. Put down 280 degrees for the art gallery."

Becky nodded and wrote down "art gallery–280 degrees" on her paper. "What about the bank?" she asked.

"Well," Amy Jo directed the compass north again. "The bank is abo-o-out 30 degrees from here," she decided, checking out her partner's sheet. "Got that down?"

"Yep," answered Becky, looking up from her paper and pencil.

"Mrs. Martin is a possibility since she keeps a lot of money hidden on her property." Amy Jo shifted the compass slightly to the right. "Forty-eight degrees for Mrs. Martin."

"Forty-eight degrees for Mrs. Martin," Becky repeated.

Amy Jo shifted her position "What else would Old Cough be interested in?"

Becky thought for a second. "Drugs at the pharmacy?"

Amy Jo looked at her friend with admiration. "Good thinking, Beck!" she said as she turned back to face Main Street. "That's just past the bank, so it would be around 30 degrees, too." Amy Jo's eyes lit up. "And . . . there are code numbers on bottles of medicine from the pharmacy, too."

"You're right!" said Becky. "Maybe the numbers we saw on that paper stand for a certain drug or something. I mean I don't know anything about it, but he might be interested in stealing drugs and reselling them."

"Hey!" Amy Jo suddenly thought of something. "They have drugs at the doctor's office."

"You mean the two Dr. Murphys?" asked Becky.

"Yeah, and it's right next to the drug store, too," murmured Amy Jo as she took that measurement. "Write down 40 degrees for the two Dr. Murphys."

"And another place that has drugs is a vet's office," Becky continued.

"Didn't think of that one," admitted Amy Jo.

"So, we'll say 265 degrees for Dr. Ullmer's office."

"Okay, 265 degrees for Dr. Ullmer," Becky repeated.

Having gathered all this information, they picked up their backpacks containing their flashlights, the black light, and extra batteries–just in case. Casting a glance over their shoulders to make sure that Ginger and Oreo were settled over at the paddock, they headed around to the front porch.

Charlotte met them at the door. Becky started in with her usual cooing noises. "How are we today, darling? Our tummy isn't upset with all that nasty medicine inside is it, hmm?"

Charlotte rubbed against Becky's leg and gave Amy Jo a cool, passing glance. The black cat had declared a truce with Amy Jo because of their mutual friend, but still maintained a safe distance.

It was really past sickening, in Amy Jo's opinion. She sniffed, but not too loudly, and pressed on into the library. She dumped all her stuff to the side of the bookcase and waited for Becky to finish giving "Darling" her medicine. She killed time by crossing over to the front window and rechecking the measurements with the compass. Everything seemed in order.

Becky joined her friend in the library, and the two girls dragged the monster chair to the bookcase. They opened the door leading to the secret passage and propped it open using the chair they decided was heavy enough to double as a truck . . . if it only had wheels. Shouldering the two backpacks, Amy Jo and Becky crawled over the chair and eased down the steps with more bravery than they actually felt. As the girls rounded the corner, Amy Jo brought out her black light and flipped it on. Becky held her chalk at the ready. Immediately, the yellow dots on the wall sprang into view. They walked through the various branches of the tunnel marking the wall with chalk every few feet. It gave the girls an increased sense of security knowing that they were not totally reliant on the aid of the black light. Somehow the tunnel had managed to shrink since yesterday. The dark walls appeared blacker. There were places where the girls had to walk single file, and other places where they could reach up and touch the ceiling with their hand. Sometimes their breath came in short, jerky gasps. They thought of turning back more than once.

The girls inched along, Amy Jo shining the light, Becky marking their passage, until they came to a section they hadn't been to the day before. These passages branched off into four different tunnels. The girls stopped short and gaped. There were florescent dots in all four tunnels. From where they stood, it was impossible to know which tunnel was the right one.

"Well, how do you like that!?" asked Amy Jo with grudging admiration. "He's made sure nobody will know which way to go from here."

"*Now* what are we going to do?" wondered Becky.

Amy Jo heaved a sigh. "Hm, why don't we try walking down each one of them for a few feet to see how far the dots go."

Becky looked doubtfully at each of the tunnels. "If we get out the compass and see which direction each one is going, we'll at least know where we're headed."

"Good idea," Amy Jo agreed as she fumbled in her backpack. She put down the black light and focused her flashlight on the compass. Facing the first tunnel, she called out its reading, "Forty-five degrees."

Becky checked her notes. "That's close to
the measurement for Mrs. Martin's house."

Amy Jo raised her eyebrows. "Let's hope he's not headed out there," she remarked. "Mrs. Martin's had enough trouble this summer." Turning to the second tunnel, she called out. "Thirty-three degrees."

"That would be the . . . bank! My Dad's there right now!"

"It's also the pharmacy and the doctors' office," Amy Jo said absently as she turned to the third tunnel. "This one is 280 degrees."

Becky rechecked her notes. "The art gallery is 280 degrees," she finally said, then jolted suddenly. "Did you hear that?" she asked looking over her shoulder.

Amy Jo stood perfectly still. Her heart rate picked up slightly as her ears strained to catch what had startled her partner. "No, what did it sound like?"

"Well . . ." It was difficult to define the noise she had heard. "A shuffling or something," was all Becky could come up with.

Amy Jo continued to listen. "Maybe it's rats."

"Oh, now I feel a *lot* better," Becky commented as she shown her light on the floor behind them.

Amy Jo decided that if they were ever going to get out of here, they'd better get back to business. "Okay, you said that 280 degrees was the art gallery, right?" asked Amy Jo as she shook her friend's arm.

"Uhhh," Becky focused her flashlight on her notes. "Right, 280 degrees is the art gallery."

Amy Jo nodded, then called out the final reading. "Okay, last tunnel . . . 260 degrees."

Becky looked up from the paper. "That's close to Dr. Ullmer's office."

"The vet," said Amy Jo as an idea suddenly occurred to her. "You know, there is something we're not even thinking about."

"What's that?"

"It's obvious," Amy Jo continued.

Becky gave Amy Jo one of her "I don't want to play this guessing game" expressions.

"There may not be steps leading up to any of these places," she explained. "I mean just because there are steps leading down from the Funderburg house, doesn't mean there are steps leading up to all these other spots as well."

Becky caught on. "Oh, I get it," she said. "Well, then, why don't we just pick one of the tunnels and see if we find any steps leading up to the surface?"

"Right," Amy Jo answered as she picked up her backpack. "No use wasting our time on passages that don't have steps leading to any of the buildings."

Since the bank, pharmacy, and doctors' office were lined up closely on the compass, they headed down the tunnel which measured 33 degrees. That way they could check out three places at once. Within a few minutes, they came upon a narrow set of steps leading upward. Unlike the Funderburg place, these steps were uneven. One step was six inches from the last step, then the very next step was ten inches higher. The passage was a tight squeeze, so the girls laid down their backpacks before climbing the first step. Flashlights in hand, they moved cautiously from one step to the next. They reached the top of the steps and before them was a door. But, whereas the door at the Funderburg house was full sized, this one was only about three feet high and two feet wide. There was no doorknob.

"Great," said Amy Jo as she stood one step below the door. "Shine the flashlight on the door so that I can use both hands to look for a catch."

"Okay," answered Becky as she focused the beam of light on the panel.

Amy Jo carefully ran her fingers over the surface of the door until her fingers felt the same slight indentation that was on the door at the Funderburg house. "This is it," she said softly as the door swung open.

Chapter 10

A Matter Of Degrees

The room was dark. In fact, it was as dark as a tomb. After they stepped through the door, the girls turned around to see exactly where the opening was located in the wall. Becky placed a chalk mark beside the tiny notch. It was disguised as one of the panels in the room.

Amy Jo motioned to Becky, and they crossed the floor to the only door. Turning the handle quietly, the girls opened it half an inch and peeked through the slit with one eye; Becky crouched down so that her head was below Amy Jo's. They saw the backs of the cashiers as they conducted last-minute business with customers. Stacks of money were at the cashiers' elbows, only a few feet from where the girls hid. The girls exchanged knowing looks.

"Where's your Dad's office from here?" Amy Jo whispered.

"It's on the second floor," Becky whispered back.

Amy Jo thought out loud. "I wonder if anybody here knows about the door in this room?"

"Dad never mentioned it at home," Becky replied. "But, maybe it's a secret, and the bank people don't want anyone else to know about it."

"Maybe," Amy Jo answered. "That kind of secret is awfully hard to keep under wraps, especially in a village like Bedford."

87

Closing the door, they retraced their steps across the floor and shone their flashlights on the panel.

After locating the chalk mark on the panel, Amy Jo pulled and pressed on the notch until the door slid noiselessly open.

Reluctantly, Becky followed her companion through the door back into the tunnel. "It definitely could be the bank," she said as she balanced herself against the narrow wall all the while trying to shine her light on Amy Jo's back.

"Could be," agreed Amy Jo, catching herself as she stumbled on the last step.

"I'm going to have to tell my Dad tonight if we think the bank's in trouble," Becky warned her friend.

"Right. No question about it," Amy Jo commented, but it was obvious her mind was moving on to new territory.

The girls leaned against the wall at the bottom of the stairs trying to decide on their next move. They looked further down the passage, which led to the drug store and doctors' office. Shrugging their shoulders they pressed on. With each passing step, the walls narrowed, and the ceiling dropped. Now, there was only room to walk single file. Flashing their lights on ahead, they could see that within another fifty feet, they would have to crawl on their knees to keep going.

Becky stopped. With a soft and shaky voice, she declared. "I think we must have passed the drug store."

Amy Jo wiped the sweat off her forehead. Her stomach was beginning to feel queasy. "You're right," she agreed. "We definitely passed it."

Without another word, both girls made an about face and retreated as fast as they could without stumbling. They didn't stop until they could walk side by side. Facing each other, the girls rested against opposite walls trying to assess their next move.

Amy Jo elbowed herself into a standing position and thought. "Okay, time to try that 280-degree tunnel and see where it takes us," she decided as she led the way.

"Isn't it about time for lunch?" Becky complained, falling in step behind. "Seems like we've been down here for hours . . . days! I mean even the army travels on its stomach, or something like that," she wasn't sure she got that phrase right, but kept plugging away on the same theme. "AWOL isn't that some army term that means 'away without official leave?' You know, when somebody leaves camp and doesn't return when he's supposed to. Well, don't be surprised if you don't see me behind you when you round the next bend," she finished with her most menacing voice. "I'll be out to lunch."

Amy Jo looked around, but decided to hold her tongue. This was not the time for well-deserved wise cracks. Instead, she silenced her friend with a short phrase. "You'd have to go back all by yourself."

Becky slumped even as she continued to walk. "Well . . . well, I can do that," she stammered. Staging a revolt could be risky. "Probably . . . maybe I could," she trotted along for another few steps, then reality hit. "This is just great! Here I am starving to death, and you want to try tunnel 280." She attempted one last plea. "Can't we at least go back to the Funderburg's house and rest for a little while. We can come back later and investigate 280."

Amy Jo stopped and studied her friend. Becky was a meltdown waiting to happen. If she didn't give her partner a break soon, Becky might never agree to come back down here again. On the other hand, it would take quite a while to get back to the house, rest, and return to this position again. "Tell you what," she began. "We pass tunnel 280 on our way *back* to the Funderburg's house. So, why don't we go down that passage for just a little ways . . . and then we'll quit until tomorrow. How's that sound?"

"Great!" Becky responded immediately. "How far arc we going to walk into that tunnel?"

"Not far," was Amy Jo's vague response. She stopped at the next branch in the passage and measured to make sure of where they were. "Yep, this one is 280."

Becky whirled around. There it was again, that same shuffling-type sound. "Did you hear that?" she asked again, only this time her voice was a whisper.

Amy Jo listened, her heart really pounding as her eyes bore into the darkness. She waited for one full minute standing close to her friend. "I don't know Becky. I don't hear anything, but I'm sure you heard something," she conceded in a quiet voice. "Let's just hurry up, check out this last tunnel, and get out of here."

Shouldering her backpack, Amy Jo gave her friend a quick look. "The flashlight only shows down there a few yards. It may not be all that long. We'll just walk a few minutes."

Amy Jo focused the black light on the fluorescing dots, while Becky shone her flashlight on the path ahead of them. Within a short period of time, the dots stopped. Something was blocking them.

The black light was stowed away in the backpack, and Amy Jo brought out her flashlight. Frowning, she placed her hand on the nearest package. "What's this?" she murmured.

Becky stepped around her friend. There were four more packages of varying sizes similarly wrapped in plain, brown, heavy paper and bound with twine. She squatted to inspect the smallest one which was only about two feet square. "Should we open them and see what they are?" she asked, completely forgetting about the strange sound she'd just heard.

Amy Jo ran her hand over the side of the package looking for a place to start. "I can't imagine what these are doing down here," she began. "But, they may be the key to the entire mystery."

"Let's open the biggest one first," said Becky as she moved to Amy Jo's side.

Amy Jo rummaged through her backpack looking for something to cut carefully through the tape holding the paper together. "I used to carry one of those Swiss Army knives with me, but I forgot to put it back in here after school was out in the spring," she scowled. "Wouldn't you just know I'd need it, too."

Suddenly, Becky remembered something. She reached in her jean's pocket and produced the knife she used to cut Charlotte's pill in half. She looked sheepishly at Amy Jo. "After I got trapped down here the first day, I decided to bring it along."

Amy Jo looked at it gratefully, but was puzzled. "How did you think it would help us?" she asked.

Becky looked a bit vague. "I don't know," she confessed. "I thought maybe we'd have to hack our way through the Funderburg door if the catch didn't work."

Amy Jo grabbed the knife and cut the twine off. Carefully, she began to cut through the tape that bound the package together, while Becky guided the flashlight just ahead of the knife. Soon, every seam had been cut through and the paper gave way. Amy Jo pulled it off. The girls leaned over and stared at what they'd found.

"How can this be?" Becky said softly. "What does it mean?"

"I got a funny feeling about this whole thing," Amy Jo muttered as she turned to the next package.

Silently, the girls opened the next four bound objects and studied the contents of each one. Standing them side by side, they looked at each in turn.

"They're all paintings we saw at the art gallery," Becky finally said. "How could they get down here?"

"I don't think they did just 'get down here'," said Amy Jo, placing the brown paper around the paintings. "I think someone is switching these pictures with the original paintings in the art gallery," she continued as she faced her friend. "Can't you see!" She grabbed her friend's arm. "That's why the pilot needed to land in a place where no one would see the plane. Even at our little air strip, someone would be suspicious of what was happening and question it later. In Bedford everyone knows everyone. If somebody we didn't know started doing something a little differently, we'd all wonder about it and ask a lot of questions."

Becky nodded her head. "That man with the raspy voice we heard at the art gallery is the same person we heard at the air strip last night!"

"Exactly!" Amy Jo agreed. "And, Cough's obviously using this tunnel to secretly trade these fake paintings with the real paintings!"

Becky sobered up. "He's using these tunnels," she repeated.

"Right!" answered Amy Jo, then understood where her friend was going with that statement. "Right," she said more softly. "He might show up any minute."

"Yeah! I know," Becky replied as she turned to make a quick exit.

Amy Jo grabbed her partner's arm. "And if  he does," she began to explain. "He might take all this stuff with him, then Officer Higgins would never believe us."

"What do you mean?" asked Becky. "This is no time to be worrying about what Officer Higgins believes. We've got to get our little ol' selves out of here."

Amy Jo picked up two of the resealed packages. "I'll take these two; you grab the other smaller ones. *Now*, we'll take our lunch break," she decided. She dug out her black light, shouldered her backpack, and aimed the black light with her remaining free hand.

Becky prayed her knees wouldn't fail her as she stumbled along. "I'm not as hungry as I was a few minutes ago," she said, shifting the paintings so that she could shine her light ahead of Amy Jo.

Amy Jo picked up her pace. "We'll take a break anyway," she said firmly. "I think we'll head for Officer Higgins' office as soon as we get out of here."

Becky nodded in relief. "Good, he's just the man I want to see right now."

They were nearly to the end of tunnel 280 when they stopped dead. It was the raspy cough again.

Chapter 11

No Exit

"I knew I heard something," Becky whispered, dropping her packages so she could grab Amy Jo's arm. "He's here."

Amy Jo stiffened as she listened for the man's next move. She could hear feet shuffling at a distance but the noise was heading their way, and he was no longer trying to keep quiet. She leaned over to Becky and whispered, "Turn off your flashlight and stay as quiet as you can."

Becky brightened suddenly. "The bank!" she exclaimed softly. "We could try the passage to the bank."

Amy Jo computed the distance in her mind then shook her head. "It's too far away. He'd nail us before we got there."

Becky leaned closer to her friend. "Maybe we could make our way quietly back to the Funderburg house with just the black light. It won't show up as much," she continued desperately.

"Listen to his footsteps, Beck. He's between us and the Funderburg house. We're not going to be able to get around him."

Becky looked at her partner in disbelief. "Well, how are we going to get out of here?" Her voice began to crack.

Amy Jo shook her head and turned back towards the passageway. "Pick up your packages and stay as close to me as you can," she said in a low voice.

That's not what Becky hoped to hear, but as quietly as possible, she stooped down, gathered the art work, and quietly fell into step behind Amy Jo.

Every noise they made seemed as loud as the garbage truck on Monday morning. The rattle of paper covering the packages was deafening. When they reached the spot where the packages had originally been stacked up, the girls stopped to think.

The sound of footsteps in the main tunnel was more distinct now.

Becky looked towards the main tunnel, then switched back to Amy Jo's face. In the black light, her friend's face looked discolored and distorted. "Well?"

Amy Jo measured her friend carefully. "There's only one thing to do," she decided. "And I just hope you're up to it."

Becky looked at her nervously, not liking the tone of her voice or the fact that a great deal might be expected of her. "Like what?" she finally said hoping her part would encompass a minor role at worst.

"We have to take him down," she answered.

"You've got to be kidding." Becky was aghast. "What if he's a three-hundred-pound gorilla? Did you ever think of that?"

"You got any better ideas?" Amy Jo said defensively. "There's no way out of here, so we have to take him down!" she said as loudly as she dared without being heard outside their immediate tunnel.

"Oh, now I get it!" Becky said, her voice rising slightly. "A karate chop to the neck using the black belt maneuver you never learned, right?"

Amy Jo placed her hand on her hip, sighed, and turned to the wall. After she had collected herself, she turned back.

"Look, we'll do it like this," she said ignoring
her partner's sarcasm. "You crouch down out
of sight beside these packages." Then Amy Jo
stopped to reevaluate her friend's level of hysteria.

Becky waited for the rest of it, then asked, "And?"

"Okay," Amy Jo continued to hesitate. "When he comes
around the corner and spots me, I'll take off, and he'll start
to chase me." She drew her breath for a second then continued. "Now, this is the tricky part."

Becky stopped her to ask, "Somehow I just know I'm
the tricky part, right?"

Amy Jo swallowed. "Well, sort of, but I know you can
do it."

"Okay, just tell me," Becky said as the sound of the
raspy cough came closer.

Amy Jo let her breath out slowly and whispered.
"You squat down here behind these packages, and I'll
take off running when he comes around the corner. Now,
when he begins to pass you, just jump out and whop him
over the head with that club over there," she finished as
she nodded towards the object on the floor."

Becky's eyes doubled in size. "Whop him over the
head!?" she whispered back.

"Right," confirmed Amy Jo.

"With that twig you call a club!?"

"Well," Amy Jo looked at the floor again, "it may not
be a club, but it's a lot bigger than a twig," she argued.

Becky thought wildly for a moment. "Why don't I run
and *you* whop him on the head?"

Air slid between Amy Jo's teeth. "Do you really think
you can run without tripping over your own two feet right
now?"

A scoff attempted an escape from Becky's throat until she realized her friend was right. She was far too shaky to run. Reluctantly she replied softly, "Okay, I'll try." Becky stumbled to her spot and squatted down out of sight. She gripped her weapon tightly in her hand and practiced striking it in the air.

Amy Jo shoved the black light in her backpack and laid it off to the side. Picking up her flashlight, she stood with her back to the main tunnel. With her head twisted looking over her shoulder, she was ready to dart when the man caught sight of her. "Ready?" she asked.

"Here's hoping," was Becky's reply.

Within seconds Cough rounded the corner. The girls saw nothing but a flashlight bobbing up and down with every footstep. Suddenly, the flashlight shone on Amy Jo's face.

"So, you found it, did you?" he asked. "Well, that's just too bad for you."

"We'll see about that!" Amy Jo yelled with more bravado than she felt.

The man moved forward, and Amy Jo shot off.

"Now, Beck, do it NOW!!" Amy Jo screamed in terror. Still she heard the man pursuing her. "Becky-y-y!"

Then there was silence except for Amy Jo's running feet. She stopped. All that could be heard were her gasps for breath. Amy Jo retraced her steps and stood over the dark heap at Becky's feet. Admiration filled her eyes. "Wow, Beck," she began. "I never thought you'd be able to do it."

Becky leaned against the wall of the tunnel but rallied enough to say, "Wasn't any big deal really."

"Ha! No big deal!?" Amy Jo patted her friend on the shoulder. "You're a hero!"

"Heroine, actually."

"Whatever," Amy Jo remembered the despicable word. "I mean you'll get written up in the Bedford newspaper."

Suddenly, the heap groaned. It was one thing to hit a moving target bent on your destruction, quite another to hit someone who was lying defenseless on the ground. Or worse yet, the heap may grab your ankle and topple you over. Cough sat between them and the main tunnel. Gradually, he sat up, picked up his flashlight, and shone it on their faces. His raspy laughter echoed through the tunnel walls. "Now we've got you."

The girls backed up. "We?" Amy Jo murmured. "There's somebody else?"

"There's a door, remember. There's a door in the fourth room of the art gallery," stammered Becky steadying herself against the wall with every step.

Amy Jo grabbed her flashlight laying on the floor. "Okay, we'll make a run for the steps," she decided. "It'll take him a minute to get to his feet."

Becky nodded. "We've got to find that door before his partner gets here."

The girls turned and raced deeper into tunnel 280. Their breath was coming in short spurts. Amy Jo tripped. Becky caught her by the arm, and they picked up speed aiming the light just a few yards ahead of their feet. The raspy laughter threatened to overtake them.

Then, suddenly another light shone ahead of them. It was a shaft of light pouring down the staircase at the art gallery. It was their escape, except a man was standing on the steps blocking their exit.

CHAPTER **12**

An Anonymous Call

A flashlight wobbled up and down as the man walked down the steps.

Forgetting their flashlights, the girls backed up, but there was nowhere to run. They heard Cough's footsteps behind them. He wasn't laughing now, just moving forward.

"Hold on there!" hollered Officer Higgins. "Just all of you hold on there!"

Cough stopped short, then turned around and began to hobble away.

"Stop him, Alan!" Officer Higgins shouted to his deputy.

Deputy Alan Howard rounded the corner into the passage and grabbed him. Cough was no match for the 6'4" deputy.

Both girls slid to the ground.

*   *   *   *

The following morning found Officer Higgins standing with Amy Jo, Becky, and Virginia Delmay in the fourth room at the art gallery. "A pretty close call if you ask me," he commented looking down the steep steps leading to the tunnel.

101

Miss Delmay turned to the girls. "But, what I don't understand is why you didn't tell me the first day you visited the gallery that someone else was back here."

"Well," Amy Jo began, "it just seemed so impossible that we heard someone so distinctly, and then he just disappeared. I mean we really looked and pounded on the wall trying to figure out where he went. I guess we decided it would be a little hard for anyone to swallow our story."

"And all that time," Becky continued, "we pounded on the wrong wall."

Amy Jo shook her head. "The entrance to the stairs was behind the *second* to last display, not the last one. We figured that the door was probably behind the last display because that's where we first heard him when we came into the room."

"But, when he got ready to leave," Becky interrupted, "he scooted around one display, opened the door, and walked down to the tunnel. We didn't hear the door open or him walk down the steps."

"He had rubber-soled shoes on, so you didn't hear his footsteps," Officer Higgins explained. "And the door is soundproof. That's why you didn't hear any noise once the door was closed."

Becky looked puzzled. "There's something I don't understand," she began. "We were so scared yesterday, we didn't even ask you how you knew we were there?"

Officer Higgins spoke up. "I got an anonymous call warning me that some girls were about to get hurt because they knew something about a tunnel leading from the art gallery . . . well, I just knew who those girls had to be," he said pointedly looking at the two young detectives.

Miss Delmay stepped in. "Were you able to trace the call? Do you have any idea who it was?"

Officer Higgins shook his head. "We don't have that kind of sophisticated equipment in a little place like this," he admitted, rubbing his short, stubby fingers together. "Anyway, there was a lot of background noise, so I suspect he was calling from a pay phone. He said that he finally decided that money wasn't going to be his boss anymore. And he hung up after telling me how to find this door."

Amy Jo cast another glance down the steps. "How did Cough know about the tunnels and what buildings had steps?"

Officer Higgins pushed his hat back on his head. "I wondered about that myself," he said. "He went to the county courthouse to look up information on the art gallery's structure. It's an historical building, so he figured there'd be some information there about it. He hoped to find access to the building through an old boarded up basement door or window. But, in studying the documents more closely, he found a series of passageways under the entire village. He dug into some old long-forgotten blueprints and discovered steps leading from the tunnel passages into some of the houses and buildings in Bedford. The tunnels were already there, but steps leading up to the houses and buildings were built during the 1800's as part of the Underground Railroad. This art gallery was one of the 'stations' where the slaves hid on their way to Canada or to safe houses."

The two girls and Miss Delmay stared at Officer Higgins in amazement. Then Amy Jo piped up. "What size shoe does Cough wear?" she asked.

Officer Higgins was taken aback. "I don't know," he answered. "I didn't check. Why?"

"Well, there's been something tickling the back of my mind for a while. We smelled cigarette smoke the first day we were at the Funderburg's house," she began. "So, the next day we did some looking around. Now, there was a size 10 pair of slippers in the upstairs closet, but all the other men's shoes were a size 12. Also, the shower liner was damp and so was one of the towels. I figured there could be several reasons for all this, but now I'm thinking that old Cough may have had something to do with it."

Officer Higgins thought about it for a moment before he replied. "I suspect when he found out the Funderburgs were leaving town, he decided to make their house his base of operations. He had to stay somewhere out of sight, and that was as good a place as any. I doubt if he realized that you girls were looking after the place, but when he found out that you came in everyday, he packed up and left."

"But he forgot to take his slippers," Amy Jo decided.

Officer Higgins nodded. "He forgot to take his slippers."

Becky leaned forward to ask a question. "The paintings just started coming in this week. It seems as though it would take a long time to plan stealing them, especially when the ones they stole had to be painted ahead of time.

Miss Delmay knew the answer to that one. "It's taken over a year to organize this show," she explained. "I've been in constant contact with several galleries and a number of artists. It was no secret that I intended to have an exhibition here in Bedford and when it was going to take place. This crime ring probably worked on the theft for the entire year." Miss Delmay was biting her lip. "This was such a close call," she shuddered. "The show opens later this week, and to think that some of the paintings on loan might have been stolen." Then, turning to Officer Higgins she asked, "Do you know anything about the thief?"

Officer Higgins scratched his sparsely-covered head. "Well, not much," he admitted. "The man these girls call 'Cough' woke up at Dr. Murphy's office. For some reason, he wouldn't give me his name even though he gave me other information. We took his fingerprints so it won't be long until we know who he is. Anyway, this is what he did tell me. There's only one person at the top of the ring who knows who everyone else is. Everyone got directions by telephone and was paid through a drop-off system. There was a source in New York at one of the galleries who told the head man what was being shipped here, so the head man paid an artist on the east coast to paint copies of some of the originals that you have on exhibit. Some fellow flew them here to Bedford. The pilot was the only one paid on the spot. Then it was Cough's job to make the switch. In fact, he was planning to make the switch tonight. Then, the pilot, whoever he is, was to fly them out tomorrow. So," he concluded, "you girls caught Cough just in time."

Miss Delmay turned to the girls. "I can't tell you how grateful I am," she said, then thought for a second. "I know what I'll do. I'll buy a month's worth of ice cream for you at Hank's Ice Cream Store. Would you like that?"

"You bet we would," said Amy Jo. "Thanks!"

"That would be great, thanks!" echoed Becky.

The following afternoon found the two detectives at Hank's Ice Cream Store cashing in on their first installment of ice cream.

Devon set the usual in front of both girls. "So, do you think they'll ever catch everybody involved with this thing?"

Becky shrugged her shoulders until she swallowed. "Don't know," she began. "Everyone in the crime ring only knew one or two other people."

"Officer Higgins thinks they'll finally get all of them," Amy added. "But, he said it may take a while. There's bound to be fingerprints on the paper wrapped around the paintings because the criminals didn't figure anyone would intercept them."

Devon leaned against the sink and looked at the girls. "The Funderburgs come back the first of the week, then you'll be out of a job."

Amy Jo nodded her head. "Looks that way," she agreed. "Guess we'll have to dig up another one."

"I've already found one," Becky announced.

Amy Jo put down her spoon and looked at her partner. "Well, aren't you the sly one," she said with an admiring tone in her voice. "So . . . what is it?"

"I go to the library every week," she began, but stopped her story to ask her friend, "do you read much?"

Amy Jo pushed her hair back. "Well, sure," she said. "But, it's mostly my Dad's collection of crime magazines and books. I scour the newspapers checking up on what's happening in the county."

"Well, the assistant librarian works only part time there," Becky continued. "Some people have a large library of books which needs to be cataloged. Now, they asked the assistant librarian to do the actual cataloging, but she needs somebody to help her get the books down off the shelves and wipe the dust off . . . that sort of thing."

"Dusting off books, you say," said Amy Jo trying not to sound too underwhelmed.

Becky nodded her head. "And if a book  looks particularly interesting, we might be allowed to borrow it and take it home to read."

"Where is it?" Amy Jo asked casually.

"Ashcroft Manor," was Becky's reply.

Devon leaned on the counter. "Hey, I hear that Ashcroft Manor is some place. I bet they have a spectacular library."

Amy Jo's interest perked up. "Ashcroft Manor," she said as she got down off the stool, and for once, did not dig in her pocket to pay for the ice cream. "Something happened there a long, long time ago, but I can't remember exactly what. Something about buried treasure, I think. A map thrown in there, too, from what I recall."

Devon and Becky stared at her for a few seconds, then Devon said, "Ah, nothing exciting ever happens at a library."

"That's what I'm counting on," answered Becky as she followed her partner out of the shop.